WINNER OF THE CARNEGIE MEDAL

GILLIAN CROSS

ILLUSTRATOR **GARETH FLOYD**

THE MINTYGLO KID

Mammoth

First published in Great Britain 1983
by Methuen Children's Books Ltd
Magnet paperback edition published 1985
Mammoth paperback edition first published 1991
Reissued 1998 by Mammoth
an imprint of Egmont Children's Books Limited
239 Kensington High Street, London W8 6SA

Text copyright © 1983 Gillian Cross
Illustrations copyright © 1983 Gareth Floyd
Cover illustration copyright © 1998 Nick Sharratt
The moral rights of the cover illustrator have been asserted.

ISBN 0 7497 0608 2

10 9 8 7 6 5 4 3 2

A CIP catalogue record for this title
is available from the British Library

Printed in Great Britain
by Cox & Wyman Ltd, Reading, Berkshire

Contents

1 · Dreadful Denzil

'There he is!' hissed Clipper. She stretched her neck and peered round the corner of the Post Office. Spag was halfway down the street, hands in his pockets, staring gloomily into a shop window full of calculators.

'Where?' said Barny. He pushed up closer to her, trying to get a look, and trod on her toe.

'Ouch!' she yelled loudly. Spag heard the noise and, with an angry glance over his shoulder, shot off down the road.

'Look what you've done, Gobbo, you clumsy oaf!' Clipper snarled.

'Me?' protested Barny. 'It was you that made all the noise.'

'Only because – oh, come *on*. He's getting away.' Gripping Barny's wrists with fierce fingers, Clipper leaped off at top speed, dragging him after her. Ahead of them, they could see Spag running, his

long, skinny legs pumping up and down in an ungainly way.

'Leggo!' Barny panted. 'Ouch – Clipper I can't – you're going too fast.'

'You shouldn't be so fat,' Clipper said heartlessly. 'Hurry up.' She hauled him over the zebra crossing, ignoring the wild hooting of the cars, and looked round. 'Where did he go?'

'Down towards the park.' Barny gulped for breath and shielded his eyes against the sun. 'Yes, look. He's down there by the pond.'

Sure enough, Spag was standing mournfully by the water, gazing at the little children sailing their boats.

'Quietly then.' Clipper put a finger to her lips. 'We'll sneak up on him.'

8

Tiptoeing elaborately, she edged through the wrought-iron gates and began to race over the grass towards the pond. Barny could not keep up with her and, when she was nearly there, he yelled, 'Wait for me!'

Spag's head jerked round and he began to run again.

'You *creep*!' Clipper bellowed over her shoulder. 'One of these days you'll fall into your mouth and drown. He's getting away.'

But Spag was no match for Clipper in a race. Halfway across the grass, she caught up with him and hurled herself forwards in a ferocious rugby tackle, hitting his legs like a small bomb. He crashed to the ground and by the time Barny got there Clipper was sitting on his back, ruffling his hair with her hands.

'Right now, Spaghetti-legs,' she said cheerfully. 'What's up? Why are you being so peculiar?'

'Don't know what you mean.' Spag rolled over, knocking her on to the ground, and sat up. 'I'm not being peculiar.'

'Oh *sure*.' Barny dropped down beside them. 'You've just been avoiding us all the week. Creeping off by yourself. That's not peculiar, I suppose. What's up?'

'Nothing.' Spag's face was long and miserable. 'I just wanted to think, that's all, and I can't do it with you two breathing down my neck. Why can't you leave me alone?'

'Leave you alone?' Clipper looked at him as if he were mad. 'But we can't leave you alone. We need

9

you. We've got to make plans. Select a team. Write out training schedules. And you're the best at that kind of thing.'

'Select a team?' Spag looked vaguely at her. 'What for?'

Clipper was speechless, and Barny had to answer for her. 'For the cricket competition, of course.'

Spag frowned, as though he were trying to remember something out of Ancient History. 'Oh yes, the Head Mister said something about it in Assembly. Hasn't it got something to do with a cricket pitch?'

'A beautiful, *proper* cricket pitch,' Clipper said dreamily. 'It belongs to some old bloke called Grimes, who owns the glue factory, and he's going to lend it to the school that wins the competition. For as long as he lives. So they can really call it their own. Imagine it. A real cricket pitch. We wouldn't have to play on the rotten bumpy grass in this park. We'd have a decent wicket and – '

' – and we've *got* to win,' Barny finished.

'Oh,' Spag said unenthusiastically. His head drooped forwards until his chin rested on his bent knees. 'Oh.'

'That's right,' Clipper said. 'Sing and dance. Give three cheers. You look about as excited as a wet kipper.'

'Can't help it,' mumbled Spag. 'Can't be excited if I'm not, can I?'

'But you *like* cricket.' Barny was surprised. 'You always say it's the only game that gives you proper sums to do. Bowling figures and batting averages and things. You were looking forward to this cricket season so you could get going with your new calculator.'

'Huh!' Spag sounded so bitter that Clipper came out of her daydreams about smooth grass and stared at him.

'What's up?'

He drooped even more. 'Fat chance I've got of getting a calculator now. The way things are, I haven't got a hope.'

Clipper finally lost her temper. Seizing his shoulders, she shook him so hard that his glasses fell off his nose on to the grass. 'James Barlow, you are the most annoying boy in the whole world. *Will you please tell us what's going on?*'

Very slowly and deliberately, Spag picked up his glasses and put them on again. 'Mintyglo toothpaste,' he said, in a voice like doom.

'Foul!' said Barny. 'But what's that got to do with anything?'

'It's my Aunt Rachel and Uncle Gregory.' Spag gave a deep sigh. 'They've won the Mintyglo toothpaste competition and they're going on a cruise to the Far East. For six weeks.'

'But that's brilliant,' Clipper said.

'Brilliant for *them*. But disastrous for me. Because they can't take Dreadful Denzil with them. So he's coming to stay with us. I've got to look after him. For *six weeks*. And my dad says I won't get my calculator unless I keep him out of trouble. But it's impossible.'

'What's Dreadful Denzil?' Barny said. 'A dog?'

'Huh!' Spag laughed sourly. 'Wish he were.'

Clipper looked hopeful. 'A boa constrictor?'

'Huh! I wouldn't care if he were a *gorilla*. A gorilla would be more human. He's my cousin and he's eight and he's worse than fifty gorillas.'

'A little kid?' Clipper sank back on her heels and shook her head. 'Honestly, Spag, you are feeble.'

'He's not a little kid,' Spag groaned. 'He's a monster from Outer Space disguised as a small boy. And not disguised very well. Look – when he was two, he poured treacle all over my bed. When he was three, he collected all the dogs in the neighbourhood and fed them our Sunday dinner.'

'And when he was four?' Barny asked with interest. But Spag only covered his face with his hands and moaned.

'I expect he's all right by now,' Clipper said confidently. 'His parents must have tamed him. That's what parents are for.'

'You don't know Uncle Gregory and Aunt Rachel. They think he's special. Every time he does something awful, they encourage him, in case it's his genius developing.'

Barny looked kindly at Spag. 'Don't worry about it. *I'll* take care of Dreadful Denzil. I'm good with little kids.' He puffed out his chest. 'What they need is kindness and a firm hand. I'll take him under my wing.'

'Quack, quack,' said Clipper. 'Gobbo the duck.'

Barny ignored her. 'Just tell me when to start. When does he come?'

Spag pulled a face. 'In about an hour. After that

12

I'll be lumbered with him and you won't want to know me.'

'Rubbish!' Barny stood up and brushed the loose grass off his trousers. 'Clipper and I will come along to meet him.'

'Hang on a minute!' Clipper scrambled to her feet. 'I can't be saddled with any little nuisances. I promised Mr Fox I'd do all the organising for the cricket matches.'

Barny looked at her severely. 'Don't be so selfish. We're Spag's friends, aren't we? Well, we ought to stand by him.'

Clipper shuffled her feet and looked sulky. 'Oh, all right,' she said at last. 'We'll come and have a look at your horrible cousin, Spag.' Then she brightened. 'But while we're going, we might as well be doing something useful. I need to talk over the team with you. Can you remember the batting figures from last year? We're going to need some really good batsmen if we get to play King's Road. That Thrasher Dyson is a really fierce bowler and I'm not sure who we've got that can stand up to him. There's Spotty McGrew, of course . . .'

She was away. Head down and hands gesturing wildly, she walked off beside Spag and for a while he forgot his troubles. Pulling a pen and a bit of paper out of his pocket, he began to make notes and argue with her.

Barny followed, but he did not attempt to join in their conversation. His head was full of quite different thoughts. He could see a Docile Denzil, tamed by clever treatment. A grateful Aunt Rachel and Uncle Gregory coming back to an amazingly well-behaved son. Saying, 'How did you do it, Barny Gobbo? We've been trying for years.'

He wouldn't boast. He'd look modest and say, 'All it needs is kindness and a firm hand.' And Denzil would look up at him adoringly ...

He was so deep in pleasant daydreams that he hardly noticed when they turned into Spag's road, until Spag gave a loud yelp.

'Yikes! They're early. That's their car pulling into the kerb. I promised I'd be there when they arrived.'

They pelted up the road towards the large, green car. As they reached it, a huge woman in a scarlet coat overflowed through the passenger door and squashed Spag into a suffocating hug.

'James, darling! How lovely to see you. How tall you're getting.'

'Ffhallo, ffAunt ffRachel,' came Spag's muffled voice from inside the hug.

'And these are your dear little friends?' Aunt Rachel turned to beam at Barny and Clipper. 'How nice of them to come along and meet Denzil.' She thrust out a fist like a great blancmange and shook their hands. Her skin was hot and damp and Clipper wiped her fingers secretly on the back of her jeans.

'Hallo, James,' said another voice. A very small man in a tweed cap had come round the car and was standing behind Aunt Rachel. 'Good to see you.'

'Hallo, Uncle Gregory.' Spag gestured at the house. 'I'll go and get Mum and Dad.'

14

But Mr and Mrs Barlow were already coming through the front door and that started another spate of hugs and kisses. Barny and Clipper stepped back to keep out of the way and Barny bumped into something solid.

'Watch where you're going, Big Bum,' said a precise, high-pitched voice.

Turning round, Barny saw what looked like a large cardboard box on legs. The box was striped in bright green and across it was written, in huge letters, MINTYGLO TOOTHPASTE, FOR MILES OF SMILES.

'Shift yourself,' said the shrill voice.

15

'Kindness and a firm hand,' Barny muttered determinedly, squashing down his urge to knock the box aside and punch the owner of the voice. Aloud, he said, 'Let me help you with that box. It must be heavy for you.'

He took the box and set it down on the ground, revealing the boy who had been hidden behind it.

He was small and thin, with a pale, freckled face and bright red hair. His teeth stuck out like a rabbit's and his ears were like jug handles. There did not seem to be anything particularly daunting about him. Barny smiled in a fatherly way.

'Hallo, I'm Barny Gobbo. And you must be Denzil.'

'Wrong again, Big Bum. I'm Batman.' The boy pulled a tube of toothpaste out of his pocket and unscrewed the cap. 'BATMAN!' Squeezing it hard, he shot a stream of bright green toothpaste all over the front of Barny's tee-shirt.

Barny gulped, trying to decide between kindness and a firm hand. But before he could say anything, Clipper's arm shot out and she wrenched the tube of toothpaste from Denzil's hands.

'I think I'd better have that.'

'Won't do you any good, Bossyboots,' Denzil said cheekily. 'I've got five years' supply in that box. It's the other part of the competition prize.'

'You wait till I tell your mum what you've done.' Clipper prodded him with a sharp finger. 'Then you'll be in trouble.'

But Aunt Rachel had already noticed. '*Darling*,'

she cooed, sweeping over to them. 'Oh Gregory, look what Denzil's done!'

Uncle Gregory turned and his eyebrows twitched with annoyance, as if he were an ordinary father. But as he opened his mouth, Aunt Rachel gushed, 'So *witty*. I know he's angry because we're going away without him, but isn't it *clever* of him to use the toothpaste to express it?'

'My mum'd wallop me if I expressed anything like that,' Clipper said.

Aunt Rachel shook her head. 'It's hard to have parents who don't understand, isn't it?' Clipper opened her mouth, to protest that she had not meant that, but she had no chance to speak. Aunt Rachel simply gushed on, like a waterfall.

'*We* understand, you see. We know that *encouragement* is what's needed for someone as sensitive as Den – as Batman.' Dropping her voice she leaned closer to Clipper. 'That's his new identity game, dear. He gets furious if you call him Denzil. Being Batman gives him a chance to express hidden parts of his personality – and we do want him to be able to express *everything*.'

'Do we?' murmured Clipper. She glanced across at Uncle Gregory.

Uncle Gregory sighed. 'It's a big responsibility for a man, having a son like Den – like Batman.'

'I'll say,' Clipper muttered. She dropped the squeezed tube of toothpaste on top of the box, flicking her fingers in disgust. At once, Denzil picked it up.

18

'I don't like you,' he announced loudly. 'You're a rotten pig.'

'Tea time,' said Aunt Rachel in a bright voice. 'Come inside, dear. I think Auntie Mary's got chocolate ice-cream.'

'I hope she's not going to let James's fat friends gobble it all up,' shrilled Denzil. 'This one's fat enough already.' He pulled a face and then, while Barny was spluttering with rage, whirled round and squirted toothpaste all over Spag's glasses.

Barny only just got to Clipper in time. She had bunched up her fists and was preparing to launch herself at Denzil. Barny clutched at her arms and held her back while the three visitors went up the path to the house.

'Stow it, Clipper,' he panted. 'You'll only get Spag into trouble. And we're supposed to be standing by him.'

'I'll stand by him OK,' growled Clipper. 'Just as long as I can stand on that little freak's head. If one of my brothers behaved like that, I'd splat him.'

'We can't splat him,' Spag said miserably. He had taken off his glasses and was trying to clean up the toothpaste with his handkerchief. 'We've got to keep him out of trouble. So Aunt Rachel and Uncle Gregory don't have to interrupt their cruise. That's what my dad said.'

'Well, I'm not going to keep him out of trouble.' Clipper frowned. 'Where he's concerned, I *am* trouble. You'd better make sure he doesn't come near me again.'

'But I can't do that.' Spag gave up his glasses as

a bad job and put them in his pocket, blinking at Clipper with his weak eyes. 'He's coming to school with me, of course.'

Clipper groaned and tore at her hair.

'Don't *worry*.' Barny patted her arm. 'I've told you. I'll deal with him. Me. Barny Gobbo.'

Clipper looked crushingly at him. 'The trouble with you, Gobbo, is you can't tell when something's too much for you.'

'He's only eight.' Barny waved a hand airily. 'I can cope with him.'

Spag said nothing. Just looked at the toothpaste on the front of Barny's tee-shirt.

'Well, I want him kept out of my way,' Clipper said firmly. 'I'm going to be very busy for the next five or six weeks. With an important cricket competition. Don't you *dare* let Denzil come interfering with that, Spag.'

'I told you you wouldn't want to have anything to do with me,' Spag muttered wretchedly.

'But I didn't – ' Clipper protested. She shook her head from side to side impatiently. 'Oh, you know what I *mean*. Make sure Denzil doesn't interfere with the competition, and I'll help you out when I'm not thinking about cricket.'

'That's never, isn't it?' Spag murmured. 'See you in six weeks, Clipper.'

'Fine friend you are,' hissed Barny.

Clipper gave a little wriggle, as though she felt awkward, and then stamped her foot. 'I think you're both being silly. I'll see you at school on Monday.'

Not bothering to wait for Barny, she marched off up the road. They could near her muttering 'Batman!' in a disgusted voice, all the way to the corner.

2 · Batman at School

'Oh, come off it, Clipper,' Barny protested. 'You're not *really* going to ignore Spag for six weeks, are you?'

Clipper stuck out her bottom lip stubbornly and kicked at the railings which ran round the playground on the school roof. 'It's his cousin, so it's his problem. Not mine.'

'But we can't leave him to cope with Denzil all by himself.' Barny looked craftily at her. 'If we do that, he won't be able to score for any of our cricket matches.'

'So?' Clipper shrugged. 'He's not the only one who can score. Spotty McGrew's little sister can do it.'

'Not like Spag. Not with all those different colours. And no one else is going to work out your batting and bowling figures for you after every match.'

Clipper kicked at the railings again, peering

down at the cars driving along the road below. 'Oh – all right,' she said at last. 'As long as it doesn't interfere with the cricket. Where are they, anyway? Spag and the little monster.'

'Over there in that big crowd. Come on. Let's go and see what they're up to.'

They trailed across the playground. Denzil was standing in the middle of a group of children, his hands in his pockets and his voice loud and bossy.

' – and when I grow up i'm going to be a really *great* crime-fighter. With a car that can go at two hundred miles an hour, and an atomic gun, and a master computer, and – '

Soppy Elaine Potter, standing on the edge of the group, gazed at him with a gooey smile. 'Oh, isn't he sweet?' she whispered to Sharon Grove. 'What a darling little boy.'

Denzil glared at her. 'I'm not a darling little boy. I'm Batman. And you're a soggy pancake.'

They all tried not to laugh. Eight year olds should not be encouraged to cheek the top class. But it was no use. One after another, they began to snigger, and then Spotty McGrew gave a rich chortle.

'He's sussed you out, Elaine. Only been here five minutes and he knows exactly what you're like.'

Then everyone was laughing. Everyone except Soppy Elaine. She tossed her head and stamped her foot at the smirking Denzil.

'No, you're *not* a darling little boy. You're a horrible, rude – '

While she was searching for a word to squelch him, there was the loud shrill of a whistle. At once,

23

everyone turned to face the centre, where Mrs Rumbelow was standing. She waved a hand for them to move into their lines.

Very elaborately, Denzil yawned and stretched.

'I'm bored with schools,' he said loudly. 'I think I'll go back to Auntie Mary's and play today.'

He set off towards the steps that led down off the roof.

'Oh *no*!' Spag groaned and buried his head in his hands. 'He's started.'

'Well, don't just let him get away with it,' Clipper spluttered. 'I'll get him.'

She raced after Denzil and caught him by the railings, seizing his arm. At once he clutched at the iron bars, anchoring himself to the spot and turning his back on her so that he was staring down at the road.

'I won't!' he shouted. 'I'm going home!'

Down on the pavement, an old man in a wheelchair was propelling himself along. At the sound of Denzil's voice he stopped and looked up, startled.

'Now then, dear.' Mrs Rumbelow had come up behind them. 'What's all this silly fuss about? Are you new?'

'He's come for six weeks.' Spag loped up apologetically. 'He's my cousin Denzil.'

'Batman!' shouted Denzil, staring down at the old man in the wheelchair. 'I'm Batman.'

'Whoever you are, the headmaster will want to see you,' said Mrs Rumbelow. 'He always sees new children starting at the school.'

Denzil smiled sweetly at her over his shoulder,

24

still gripping the railings. 'But I'm not starting at the school. I'm going back to Auntie Mary's to play.'

'Don't be silly.' Mrs Rumbelow took off her glasses to peer more closely at him. 'Surely you're not *frightened*? A big boy like you?'

'Course I'm not frightened,' Denzil yelled. 'Batman's never frightened. I just don't want to go to school.'

The old man in the street was chuckling now, his head tilted back to look up at them. Must seem pretty funny, thought Barny. One little boy standing out against the crowd of people all round him.

But Mrs Rumbelow did not think it was funny. She frowned down at the old man and then slapped

Denzil's hands, hard, so that he let go of the railings with a whimper. Clipper seized them immediately.

'No more nonsense, now,' said Mrs Rumbelow severely. 'James, take him down to the headmaster at once.'

'Yes, Mrs Rumbelow,' muttered Spag as she turned away.

Denzil ground his teeth and hissed, 'Rotten old crow! I'll KAPOW your glasses for you.'

One or two of the children giggled, but Clipper shook him furiously. 'You lousy little creep. If you get Spag into trouble, I'll make you into sausages.'

Barny pulled a face at her. She obviously did not understand how to deal with little kids. Smiling kindly, he took Denzil's arm.

'Come on. We'll take you down to the Head Mister. He's not frightening. Just a bit daft. We'll look after you.'

'I can look after myself, Big Bum,' said Denzil, wriggling away. But he had worked out that there were too many of them to fight. Sulkily, he made for the door that led down into the school, muttering, 'I'll get my own back on that stuffy old teacher. *No one* smacks Batman.'

'Phew!' Spag wiped his forehead. 'I told you what he was like. I'll be worn down to the bone by the end of six weeks.'

'That'll be nice,' murmured Clipper. 'Then you'll be able to slide down drainpipes. Oh, come on, you two. Let's get that little beast to the Head Mister. Then we can forget about him and do

26

something *important*. I've got to talk to Mr Fox about cricket practices.'

But it was not so easy to forget about Denzil. All through the day, Barny found himself worrying over the problem. What could they do to keep him out of trouble? He tried to discuss it with Spag and Clipper, but they were no use. Spag was deep in a complicated problem about seven bulldozers moving six hundred tons of earth at different speeds. Every time he had a moment to spare, he took it out and worked on it a bit more. And Clipper was no better. She was drawing an elaborate plan of a cricket pitch, showing all possible fielding positions, neatly labelled.

They're hopeless, thought Barny, as they sat in the last lesson of the day. *Hopeless. Once they get wrapped up in something, they don't take any notice of what's going on.*

Then it burst on him. That was the answer! If Denzil could be like that, he wouldn't have any time left to cause trouble. What they had to do was find something that would take up all his attention. Like sums for Spag and sport for Clipper. Barny was so excited that he stared impatiently up at the clock, waiting for the hands to reach three-thirty so that he could get out of the classroom and find Denzil.

But as soon as they came out of the door at the end of the day, it was obvious that there was something wrong. Down by the cloakrooms, a little group of children had gathered. They were gazing

27

down at the ground, whispering and poking each other. Soppy Elaine Potter was just ahead of Barny, Spag and Clipper and, as she reached the group, she gave a delighted gasp of horror.

'Oooh, look! Look, Sharon, how terrible. It must be Spag's horrid cousin that's done it.'

Spag yelped and lolloped down the corridor, pushing everyone else out of the way with his pointed elbows. Giving an exaggerated groan, Clipper sprinted after him and, by the time Barny panted up, the two of them were in the centre of the circle of children, gaping down at the floor.

There was no sign of Denzil himself. But there on the tiles lay Mrs Rumbelow's glasses. The frames were splintered apart and the lenses lay shattered into hundreds of pieces, as though someone had stamped on them hard with the heel of a shoe.

Beside them was a curling trail of green toothpaste that spelt out a single word. BATMAN.

'Disaster!' moaned Spag.

Clipper pressed her lips together and thudded her fist into her other hand. 'Just wait till I catch that little fiend!'

Soppy Elaine wriggled her shoulders happily. 'There's going to be the most frightful trouble. I expect the Head Mister will come round to see your mum, Spag. They're bound to know it's Denzil. We all heard him say he'd kapow Mrs Rumbelow's glasses, and someone's sure to tell . . .'

'Yes?' murmured Clipper. She did not say any more. Just looked down at her fists. But Soppy Elaine turned pale and took a step backwards.

Barny decided it was time to take charge. 'I don't know why you're all wasting time arguing. We've got to get this lot cleared up before anyone comes. Give us a hand. We'll put all the bits in my bag.'

They began to scoop up the broken plastic and sweep the splinters of glass into a piece of paper. As they bundled it all up and thrust it into the bag, Spotty McGrew glanced over his shoulder.

'Watch out! Here comes the Rumbelow.'

Spag looked round wildly at everyone. 'Please don't tell her.'

'Course not,' said everyone. Except Soppy Elaine. She smiled a satisfied little smile, like a cat's, and pointed at the floor.

'We don't need to tell her, do we? As soon as she sees that, she'll know Denzil's been up to something.'

The straggle of toothpaste was still there, spelling out the tell-tale word.

There was no time to wipe it up. Mrs Rumbelow was already halfway down the corridor. And there was no chance that she would not notice the bright green letters. Even without her glasses, she could not miss them.

Barny acted instantly, while everyone else was still gasping. Without any hesitation, he plumped down on to the floor, planting his bottom squarely on the toothpaste letters and hiding them completely.

'Eugh!' said Soppy Elaine. 'I don't know how you can – '

Clipper trod on her toe and she shut up.

'Barny Gobbo!' Mrs Rumbelow pushed her way through the group and stared down at him. 'What on earth do you think you're doing?'

'Resting, miss.' Barny looked innocently up at her.

'*Resting?*'

'Yes, miss.' He gazed earnestly into her eyes. 'We've been doing fiendish sums, all about bulldozers moving earth and digging ditches. The thought of all that work! It's made me absolutely exhausted.' He gave a huge yawn.

'You're talking nonsense, boy. Get up off the floor at once.'

'I will in a minute. Honest, miss. Just let me get a bit more energy first.'

She peered down at him, her weak eyes blinking. 'You haven't been fighting, have you?' Glancing

30

round, she picked on Spag, because he was standing separately from the others. 'James, did you knock him down?'

'I wouldn't fight *Spag*,' Barny interrupted, sounding quite shocked. 'He's got glasses.'

Mrs Rumbelow looked vague for a moment, like someone who has been reminded of something. 'Oh yes. That's what I was doing when I came along. Has anyone seen my glasses? The old ones with the blue frames?'

Soppy Elaine opened her mouth and everyone glared at her.

'So *that's* it, miss!' Spotty McGrew smacked his hand against his forehead. 'I knew there was something different about you.'

'Perhaps you left them in the staffroom,' Clipper said helpfully.

'Ah.' Mrs Rumbelow brightened. 'Yes. Now I come to think of it, I did take them off at lunchtime to do the crossword. Perhaps someone put something down on top of them.'

'Don't you think you ought to go and look, miss?' Spag said. 'Before someone sits on them.'

For a moment Mrs Rumbelow looked suspiciously round at them all. Then she sighed. 'Yes, I'd better. It's annoying to lose them, because I don't get my new ones until next week.' She turned and began to walk off down the corridor, calling over her shoulder, 'And *do* get up off the floor, Barny. You're making the place look untidy.'

As soon as she was safely round the corner, Barny began to peel himself off the floor.

31

'YUCK!' said everyone as the patch of squashed toothpaste appeared. Soppy Elaine turned away, wrinkling her nose.

'You are disgusting, Gobbo.'

'Charming,' Barny said, in an injured voice. 'You wouldn't think I'd saved the situation, would you? Don't you realise that Spag would be in a terrible row by now if I hadn't used my brains?'

'So *that's* where you keep your brains,' murmured Spotty McGrew.

Barny turned away haughtily and pulled his PE shorts out of his bag. Crumpling them up, he went down on his hands and knees and began using them to wipe the rest of the toothpaste off the floor.

As he removed the last smear, a precise, shrill voice said from behind him, 'You do look funny. There's a great splodge of green on your trousers. Just as if you'd sat in some toothpaste.'

Grinding his teeth, Barny straightened up and whipped round. Denzil was looking calmly at him, with a little smile on his face. For a moment, no one could speak.

Then Barny said fiercely, 'Don't you realise that you almost got Spag into the most appalling row? You deserve to be shut up in a cupboard for a week and fed on spiders. And when I get my hands on you – '

'Kindness and a firm hand,' murmured Clipper naughtily. 'That's all it takes to deal with little kids.'

Barny gulped. He had forgotten all about his great scheme for managing Denzil. And it would

32

never work if he quarrelled with him. So he forced a sickly smile on to his face.

'Anyway,' he said, in a sugary voice, 'it's been really good fun. We had a real laugh. Pity you missed it.'

'I was busy,' Denzil said. 'I was practising singing in the Boys' toilets.' He let out a raucous screech. 'See? I haven't got a bad voice, have I? I think I ought to make a record.'

'Yeah,' Spotty McGrew said sarcastically. '*Batman Sings Boogie*. Really wild.'

Barny ignored all the others, who were sniggering at Spotty's joke. This was his chance! He seized it.

'That's not a bad idea Den – I mean Batman. Course, you'd need a manager, wouldn't you? Someone to work on your image and write to record companies and help you practise. You'd need lots and lots of practice, of course. It would probably take up most of your time.'

Putting an arm round Denzil's shoulders, he walked away up the corridor with him, talking all the time.

'Don't they look *sweet*!' cooed Soppy Elaine.

'Sick, sick, *sick*!' Clipper rubbed her forehead. 'Do you think Gobbo's gone mad, Spag?'

Spag's face drooped gloomily. 'Nope. I think it's worse than that. I think he's got an Idea.'

They looked nervously at each other. Barny's Ideas had a way of causing big trouble.

'Perhaps he'll forget about it,' Clipper said hopefully. 'After all, he'll have plenty to take his mind

33

off it when his mum sees his trousers and his PE shorts.'

'Clipper,' said Spag. 'Have you ever known anything get in the way of one of Barny's Ideas? Even his mum?'

All the same, they were slightly comforted when they passed Barny's house on the way home. Mrs Gobbo's voice could be heard all across the scrapyard and out in the street.

'... and you'll wash them and scrub them until they *are* clean, Barny Gobbo! Then I'll think what I'm going to do to punish you. You needn't think you can go rolling in toothpaste and come home as if nothing had happened! I ought to take the frying pan to your backside! Shut you out in the scrapyard all night! If I'd behaved like that to my mother ...'

Spag grinned. 'She'll be at it for another hour at least. I don't think Gobbo will get up to anything else today.'

They crept quietly past the scrapyard gates.

3 · 'Ya Godda Have ROCK!'

'You've got to come!' Spag heaved at Barny and Clipper, tugging them along the road. 'Six days it's been going on, nearly. Since Monday night. And it's all Gobbo's fault. You just come and see how bad it is.' He hauled them round the corner into his road. 'There,' he said bitterly. 'You can even hear it from here.'

His house was about halfway down, but even from where they were standing the noise was unpleasantly loud. A terrific crashing and banging. As they walked towards it they heard, over the top of that noise, a curious high-pitched whining.

'Ya godda have ROCK!' (*bang, crash, boom*)

'Ya godda have ROLL!' (*boom, bang, crash*)

'What *is* it?' Clipper said. 'What's the clattering noise?'

'Saucepans.' Spag sighed. 'He decided that he needed drums to accompany his singing. He told Mum that Aunt Rachel and Uncle Gregory would have bought him a set straight away, to encourage his talent. Mum said she couldn't afford that, and she gave him the saucepans instead.'

'But why does she let him do it?' Barny tried to imagine his own mother putting up with the awful racket for five minutes. The thought almost made him smile.

'She tried stopping him.' Spag shuddered. 'He just lay on the floor and went purple in the face and screamed and screamed until we all thought he was going to choke to death. And Mum was afraid that if it went on she'd have to get Aunt Rachel and Uncle Gregory to come home.'

'But don't the neighbours complain?' said Clipper.

'All the time,' Spag said, looking glum. 'It wasn't quite so bad in the week, because it was only for an hour or so before he went to bed, but now it's Saturday, there's no end to it.'

They were standing outside the house by now. Clipper shrugged and looked up at the window of the front bedroom.

'Well, *I'm* not staying here to listen to it. Gobbo and I have to get down to the park. The match starts in half an hour. The first one of the competition. We were hoping you could come down and score.'

'Oh, I can come,' Spag said wryly. 'If I bring Denzil. And his drums.'

'*Oh* no,' Clipper spluttered. 'I'm not having that little monster anywhere near my cricket match.'

'That's not fair,' Barny protested. 'At that rate, Spag's going to miss all the matches.'

'I can't help that,' Clipper said firmly, raising her voice above the clatter of the saucepans. 'I want to win that cricket pitch and *I will not have a freak like Denzil interfering*!'

Abruptly, the noise stopped and there was an angry shout from the house. The window flew open and Denzil's head poked through it. He was just about recognisable. Long streaks of green toothpaste had been drawn down his cheeks and there was a green blob on the end of his nose. Clipper let out a yelp of laughter and he thumped the window frame crossly.

'Be *quiet*! You're making so much noise I can't hear myself practise.'

'Surprised you can hear anything through all that toothpaste,' grinned Clipper. 'What's the matter? Couldn't you find your mouth?'

Denzil looked haughtily down at her. 'That's my face paint. Singers have to think about their image as well as their songs. That's what Big Bum told me.'

'Oh, well done, Gobbo,' Spag murmured. 'I told you it was all your fault, didn't I?'

Barny ignored him. He was used to being misunderstood. Even Spag and Clipper did not always grasp the brilliance of his ideas. And it was not his fault Denzil had turned out to be such a rotten singer. It was just a pity he didn't realise how ear-scorching his voice was. If only he could hear himself . . .

That was it! Flinging his head back, Barny shouted up at the window. 'You're doing fine! But you know what you ought to do next?'

Denzil leaned further out of the window, looking interested, and Barny smiled at him.

'You ought to get hold of a tape recorder and do a test recording. That's how all the best singers started out. Then you can hear how you sound to other people.'

Denzil did not answer. But he nodded thoughtfully and drew his head back in, shutting the window.

'That should fix him,' Barny said smugly.

'Fix him?' Spag raised his eyebrows. 'Honestly,

Gobbo, did you leave your brains in the wash? Don't you realise – '

But Clipper had had enough of talking about Denzil. Without waiting to hear what Spag had to say, she seized Barny's tee-shirt and began to drag him away, towards the park.

'Do you want to miss the match? Canberra Green'd love that. They don't stand any chance of winning if we all turn up. Oh, come *on*, Gobbo.'

Struggling, Barny twisted his head round and shouted back over his shoulder, 'It'll be OK. You wait and see. I've solved it.'

But Spag did not even look as though he had heard. He was staring miserably up at the window, where the clattering had begun again.

'Five wickets!' Clipper said gleefully. 'I've never taken so many in one match. The last one was the best. As soon as the ball left my hand, I knew – '

Barny and Spag sighed and looked at each other. She had been going on like that ever since Saturday and she looked set to carry on right through dinner break without drawing breath. Hugging her knees, she leaned back against the chimneystacks in their special corner of the playground and gazed at the sky as she re-lived every moment of the match.

'Good thing you *were* bowling well,' Spag interrupted her. He had the scorebook in his hands and was frowning as he looked down at it. 'Because our batting was lousy.'

'*I* was OK,' Barny said defensively. 'I got five. That's not bad for a wicket-keeper.'

'And you were nearly top scorer except for Clipper and Spotty McGrew,' Spag pointed out. 'The others were disgusting. You may have been able to scrape by against Canberra Green, but you'd never beat King's Road like that. Not with Thrasher Dyson bowling.'

Clipper suddenly looked sour. 'He was there on Saturday. Spying. Spent the whole match chewing gum and sniggering at us.'

'I'm not surprised.' Spag jabbed a finger at the scorebook. 'You've got to *do* something about this, Clipper. How about holding batting trials for the Third Years? There must be someone there who'd be some use.'

Clipper looked up, interested, but before she could say anything a sugary voice broke in.

'Oh, *here* you are. I've been looking everywhere for you.'

Clipper groaned elaborately. 'No, it's not us. It's a gang of muggers disguised as us. So you'd better run away before we scrag you.'

Soppy Elaine giggled nervously. 'Honestly, Clipper, it's *boring* the way you're always joking. And I'm only trying to help. I came to tell you about Spag's cousin.'

They all sat up sharply and looked at her and she smirked. 'I mean – he is making rather a lot of *noise*. He said it was all Gobbo's idea. But I didn't believe him, of course. Even Gobbo couldn't be as stupid as that.'

'Elaine,' Spag said, with quiet fury, 'will you please tell us *what Denzil's doing?*'

40

'We – ell – ' Elaine spun it out as long as she dared, enjoying herself. 'He's in the Hall with a crowd of little kids. And he's got a crate of empty milk bottles and the lids from the dinner ladies' saucepans and a tape recorder from the Head Mister's office and – '

Her voice faded away as the three of them pushed past her and raced for the stairs down into the school, ignoring her as she followed behind chattering.

'I hope we're not too late,' panted Spag.

The Hall had heavy wooden doors that shut in the sound. When Spag pushed them open, a hideous din floated out. The crashing of metal mixed with the tinkling of glass. And above it all wailed Denzil's voice.

'Ya godda have ROCK!' (*bang, crash, boom!*)

'Ya godda have ROLL!' (*boom, bang, crash!*)

'Ya godda have the

BATMAN rock'n'roll!' (*bang, boom, crash, crash, crash!*)

He was standing on the stage, waving his arms about like a conductor as he sang. On one side of him were three little boys, each holding two of the huge metal lids that covered the saucepans in the school kitchen. They were crashing them together like giant cymbals.

On the other side, a lot of milk bottles had been arranged in a line. Each one held a different amount of water. Two little girls knelt behind them, tapping them with pencils to make a rough tune.

'Denzil!' thundered Spag, in a terrible voice. 'What are you doing?'

The noise faltered and stopped. Denzil gave a cheerful grin. 'Isn't it lovely? I'm doing what Big Bum told me to. I'm making a test recording. And this is my band.'

'Oh yes?' said Clipper. 'And I suppose Mr Pratt *said* you could have the empty milk bottles? And Mrs Mitchell *kindly* gave you the saucepan lids?'

'Not *exactly*.' Denzil shuffled his feet. Then he brightened. 'But I'm sure they would've. If they knew I needed them for my development.'

Barny was staring at a chair on the edge of the stage. Marching towards it, he pointed a finger. 'And what's that?' It was a small cassette tape recorder, whirring away.

'That's a tape recorder,' said Denzil.

'I know that.' Barny tried to sound patient. 'But where did you get it from?'

'Oh, it was on the desk in the Head Mister's office,' Denzil said airily. 'But he won't worry. I left a sign to show it had been taken by a good character. I wrote – '

'Oh no!' Spag buried his face in his hands. 'What are we going to *do*?'

'We'll have to take all the stuff back,' Clipper said firmly. 'Before there's trouble.'

Denzil gave a loud howl. 'But what about my recording session? We haven't finished.'

'Oh yes you have.' Clipper glanced round at the little boys and girls. 'Because your band's going to run away. Now. Or there'll be big trouble. Scat, you lot.'

They took one look at her and scatted.

'Right,' said Barny. 'Now we must get rid of this lot.'

There was a little snigger from behind them. 'You're bound to get caught. You're not even supposed to be in the school in dinner break.'

They had forgotten about Soppy Elaine. She was standing in the doorway, looking smug. Clipper gave her a sugary smile, with bared teeth.

'Ever been under a steam roller, Elaine? It's a good way of slimming. Perhaps I'll help you try it.'

Soppy Elaine yelped and fled and they turned back to sorting out the things.

Spag and Clipper carried the milk bottles in their crate, tiptoeing along the corridor to the caretaker's office. Through the half-open door, they could see Mr Pratt munching his way through a huge pile of cheese sandwiches. Very carefully, so as not to attract his attention, they pushed the crate along until it was in front of the door. Then they started to sneak back towards the corner.

They were almost there when Spag suddenly sneezed. There was a yell from the caretaker's office.

'You kids ought to be *outside*!'

Clipper seized Spag's arm and dragged him round the corner, just as they heard the office door open wide. Then there was a loud, disastrous clatter and a crashing of glass. Peering back down the corridor, they saw Mr Pratt sitting on the floor rubbing his elbow. Beside him was the milk crate he had tripped over and all round lay bits of broken bottle.

'Vanishing time,' whispered Clipper.

Barny did not think he could sneak the lids back into the kitchen without being noticed. There were six of them and he could hardly get his arms round the pile. So he made a different plan. Putting them carefully down beside the door, just out of sight, he sauntered into the kitchen, sniffing at the clouds of delicious steam.

Mrs Mitchell, the school cook, advanced towards him. She was a little woman, like a weasel, and she hated children.

'Out!' She pointed at the door.

Barny sniffed again. 'It's the smell,' he said longingly. 'You're such a *brilliant* cook, Mrs Mitchell. Can't I have a bit of dinner now?'

'All you'll get is a knuckle sandwich, my lad.' She shook her fist at him. 'Out! There's enough people in this kitchen already.'

'Oh!' Barny let a great smile of understanding break over his face. 'Is that why you've put the saucepan lids outside? To make more room?'

'What?' She took a step towards him, looking puzzled, and he backed away. 'You wait a minute, Barny Gobbo. What do you mean?'

'No, it's all right. Honest.' He edged quickly through the door. 'I can wait until my proper dinner time. Even if I am starving to death.'

She made a grab for him but he slid away up the corridor. As she followed him, she cannoned into the pile of lids. The last Barny saw, as he glanced over his shoulder, was the sight of lids rolling

everywhere, like cartwheels, and Mrs Mitchell panting backwards and forwards trying to catch them.

'Phew!' he gasped as he reached the Head Mister's office, where Clipper and Spag were waiting outside the door. 'I'll be glad when this is over. Why haven't you got rid of the tape recorder yet?'

Spag glanced nervously at the closed door. 'But suppose he's *inside*?' he whispered.

Barny looked at him scornfully. 'What's up? Are you scared? I'll knock on the door. If he answers, I'm sure I'll be able to think up a story. That's the good thing about having quick wits.'

'Your wits couldn't win a race in the Snails' Olympics,' Clipper said. But she didn't sound as rude as usual. She was happy enough to let Barny do the knocking and she held her breath like the others, waiting for an answer.

But there was no answer.

'See?' Barny pushed the door open. 'Good thing one of us has got some sense. Now let's get rid of that recorder.'

Clipper rushed in and put it down on the desk, but Spag shook his head.

'Not there, dumbo. If he *has* missed it, he'll know it's been put back since he went out. If we hide it, he might just think he's made a mistake. Let me see – '

He slid it on to the windowsill, so that it was almost completely hidden by the curtain, and then he turned round.

'Crumpets!'

'What's up?' Clipper said impatiently. 'It's time we got out of here.'

'But we can't go yet. Look.' Spag pointed at the large oval mirror which hung on the wall beside the door. Across its gleaming surface sprawled tooth-paste letters, five inches high.

BATMAN.

'We'll *have* to get rid of that,' Spag said desperately.

Clipper clenched her teeth and began to mutter about wooden-headed little monsters, but Barny strode across to the mirror, pulling out a large, grimy handkerchief.

'No good dithering. We must just clean it off.'

He began to scrub away at the toothpaste, smearing it into a squelchy green blur. His handkerchief soaked it up and turned green, but it did not seem to get any less. It just slurped round and round, working its way up his fingers and over his wrist and covering more and more of the mirror.

And then a voice behind them said, 'Just what do you three think you're doing?'

Clipper jumped and Spag jerked round. But Barny did not move as quickly as they did. By the time he had turned to face the headmaster, he had had time to think.

'We're cleaning your mirror, sir.'

'*Cleaning* my mirror?' The headmaster raised his eyebrows.

'Yessir.' Barny nodded and rubbed his toothpastey hand across his forehead. 'It was really awful. Fingerprints everywhere. Made your office look dis-

47

gusting. But we're using this smashing new cleaner. It's called – er – Mirrorglo, and it's really fantastic – '

'Yes, yes, spare me the commercials.' The headmaster flapped a hand to shut him up. 'Are you really asking me to believe that you – *you* Barny Gobbo – are missing your dinner just to clean my mirror?'

Barny hesitated for a fraction of a second. Then a smile of innocent surprise spread over his face. 'Goodness me, sir, is it time for Second Dinners already? I never noticed. It just shows how quickly the time goes when you're enjoying yourself.'

The headmaster gave a curious splutter and looked at them all suspiciously for a moment. Then he nodded. 'I see. Well, since you enjoy it so much, you'll be quite happy to come back in afternoon break and finish it off, won't you?'

'Yes sir.' Barny gulped.

'And since you're all so keen on cleaning,' the headmaster went on, smiling cheerfully, 'I'm sure you'd like to give the windows a rub and get a brush and dustpan and do the floor as well. Eh? Caroline? James?'

'Yes sir,' they chorused meekly.

'Good. Now get along and have your dinners.'

As soon as the door closed behind them, the other two leaped on Barny.

'Gobbo, you are *dumb*,' hissed Clipper. 'Now we've got to miss all our break slaving away over his beastly room.'

48

Barny looked injured. 'I thought you'd be grateful. I think I got us out of that very neatly. At least he didn't discover what we were really up to.'

'Let's just hope,' drawled Spag, 'that he doesn't decide to lick his mirror before we get back. If he finds out what's on it, he'll really start asking questions.'

'That's all right,' said Barny. 'I'll think of something. I told you I had quick wits.'

Clipper grinned suddenly. 'Oh, I'm glad about that,' she murmured.

Barny nodded. 'So you should be. I've always told you that you don't realise how lucky you are to have a friend as brilliant as me. Now you know.'

'Oh yes,' Clipper said, even more softly. 'I'm really pleased about your quick wits.'

Barny looked suspiciously at her. 'What are you on about?'

Clipper's grin widened. 'Well, you're going to need *really* quick wits when you get home tonight, aren't you?'

Spag spluttered, as though he had just seen a joke, and Barny glared at him.

'Why don't you stop fooling about and tell me?'

Clipper pointed gravely to the soggy green handkerchief he was still clutching in his hand, and the long green smears that ran up the sleeve of his school shirt.

'Your mum's going to want to know why you've come back from school with your clothes covered in toothpaste. For the second time. If I were you, I'd start thinking up a good story now.'

Even Spag laughed out loud at the expression on Barny's face.

4 · The Great Artist

'Right now, you kids.' Clipper stood in the middle of the park and looked along the row of Third Years in front of her. 'It's batsmen we need. We've had two matches in this competition so far and each time we've just scraped by on our bowling. So if you turn out to be any good, you'll be in the team. OK?'

They nodded and she spat on her hands and rubbed them together.

'This is what we're going to do. I'll bowl six balls at each of you and see how you do. If you miss them all, you're out for sure. And if you run away – well, you can keep running for all I care. But if you manage to hit some of them Spotty and Gobbo will be watching you to see how you shape up and who's got the best style.'

The Third Years nodded again. There were twelve of them, nine boys and three girls, and they all looked slightly daunted as Clipper picked up the

51

ball and tossed it from hand to hand, frowning ferociously.

'Who's first, then? How about you Toby Jackson?'

Toby, a short, fair-haired boy, shuddered as though he wanted to give up straight away, but the others pushed him forward and Clipper grinned encouragingly.

'Here, you can borrow my bat if you like. But if you don't take care of it I'll skin you. It's my new one. Now get down there and help Spotty stick in the stumps. The rest of you can field.'

She pulled a face at Barny. 'That's the worst of playing in this wretched park. If you don't get to the ball fast enough, some silly little kid walks off with it.'

Waving her hands, she began to order them all into their places.

'I can't stand bossy girls, can you, Sharon?' said an irritating voice behind her. 'It's so – unfeminine.'

Clipper turned round and glared. Soppy Elaine and Sharon Grove were out in the road, smiling sweetly through the railings.

'I should push off, if I were you,' Clipper said crossly. 'You don't want to get a ball in the face, do you?'

But the railings in between obviously made Soppy Elaine and Sharon feel brave. They simply smirked and lounged against the fence, watching. Clipper bared her teeth at them and turned away in disgust, but before she could walk down to begin

52

bowling she heard another, even more unwelcome voice from the other side of her.

'I've decided to forgive you. Because you need me.'

'*What?*' Clipper spun round. Denzil was standing there, looking completely self-possessed.

'I'm a brilliant batsman,' he said loudly. 'There never was a batsman as good as me. I don't know why you're bothering with all those others when you could have – '

'Spag,' Clipper yelled, seeing him come lolloping across the grass, 'will you get your disgusting cousin out of here!'

'Sorry, Clipper,' Spag panted apologetically. 'He got away. We were in the Library and I just happened to mention what you were doing this morning. Then I found a really good book on computer programming and when I looked round, he'd gone.'

'She ought to let me be in her cricket trials,' Denzil said, beginning to look sulky. 'It was nice of me to come and be friends after she was so beastly about the tape recorder, and I'm just what she needs for her team, and – '

'Ah!' cooed Soppy Elaine from the other side of the fence. 'Poor little boy. How can you be so mean to him, Clipper?' The unbelievably innocent look on her face showed how much she was enjoying herself.

'*Spag!*' yelled Clipper. 'I'm trying to hold a serious cricket trial. Will you take that awful little monster away before – before I EAT him!'

53

Barny had seen the argument from a distance and now he came lumbering up the slope, puffing importantly. Denzil had planted his feet firmly apart and was looking as though he would have to be carried away.

'Leave this to me,' Barny hissed under his breath. Turning to Denzil, he forced a kindly smile on to his face.

'Look, Batman, we're only testing Third Years. And it's likely to be a bit rough. You've never seen Clipper bowling, have you? She's really fierce. If I were you, I'd go away and do something nice and peaceful like – ' he racked his brains quickly ' – like painting.'

'*Painting?*' said Denzil, as though he were about to be sick.

'Yes.' Barny waved his arms about enthusiastically. 'That's a nice, quiet job. And if you're good, you could be famous. Even after your death. Not to mention the money you'd make. Some artists make lots and lots of money and – '

An odd, distant look had come into Denzil's eyes. Suddenly, without any warning, he turned round and raced away across the grass.

'What have you done *now*, Gobbo?' groaned Spag.

'Saved the situation, as usual,' Barny said stiffly. 'You might say thank you.'

But Spag was already racing away after Denzil.

'At least *you'll* be pleased,' Barny said, looking hopefully at Clipper. But she only sighed impatiently.

54

'All I want to do is get on with this cricket trial. Get down there with Spotty and watch, Gobbo.'

Muttering under his breath, Barny plodded down towards the edge of the pitch and Clipper, in a rage, walked backwards to begin her run-up. Because the park was crowded on Saturday mornings, she had to start at the top of the slope, and she came hurtling forwards, grinding her teeth and snorting through her nostrils.

The sight of her was too much for Toby Jackson. He took one look, dropped the bat and ran away.

'What a weedy lot!' Clipper said in disgust, as she and Barny walked home along the High Street. 'One of them ran away, six missed every ball and two of them wouldn't even have a go at facing the bowling. The only one who was any good was Jimmy Brown.'

'You should have let me bowl,' said Barny. 'You just scared them. You looked as though you wanted to cannonball them into the ground.'

'Well, that's what it's going to be like,' Clipper snorted. 'If they can't face me, what're they going to do if we meet King's Road? Thrasher Dyson is a much faster bowler than me. *And* bigger. *And* rougher.' She made a mock swing with her bat.

Barny hung his head gloomily and pushed his hands into his trouser pockets. 'We'll be lucky to get as far as playing King's Road, won't we? We've got to win the match this afternoon first, and even if we do get Jimmy Brown to play – '

55

He broke off as he saw a familiar figure come flying across the High Street, arms and legs flailing. As he reached them, he skidded to a stop.

'You are dumb, Spag,' said Clipper. 'You're supposed to use the subway to cross the road here. Didn't you hear all those cars hooting at you?'

'No time for stuff like that.' Spag panted and waved his arms at them. 'Had to get to you quickly. You've got to help me.'

Clipper groaned. 'What's the matter now?'

'It's Denzil – '

'Don't want to know,' Clipper said obstinately.

'But I've lost him. I mean, I've really lost him.'

'Oh, well *done!*'

'Don't be so rotten, Clipper.' Barny gave her a shove. 'Tell us what happened, Spag.'

Spag gulped to get his breath back. 'I caught him up quite soon after he ran away from the cricket. I thought he'd be in an awful temper, ready to throw one of those frightful screaming fits of his. But he wasn't. He said he'd decided you didn't deserve to have him in your team.'

'Good,' muttered Clipper.

Barny kicked her. 'Go on, Spag.'

'Well,' Spag said more slowly, 'he told me he had decided to be an artist, like you said, Gobbo, because he wanted to earn money to save up and buy a Batmobile. And when we got home, he went up to his room and shut himself in. So I went off to read my book on computer programming in peace.' His attention wavered for a moment. 'It's a really good book. Did you know – '

56

'Oh, get on with it,' Clipper said impatiently. 'What happened next?'

'That's just it.' Spag frowned. 'I don't really know. When Mum sent me up to tell him lunch would be in half an hour, he wasn't there. I didn't dare tell Mum he'd gone, so I came out to try and find him. And I got on OK at first. I kept meeting kids from school who'd seen him. But when I got as far as this, the trail just seemed to run out.'

'Best thing,' said Clipper. 'It'd be an awful shame if you found him.'

'But that's no good,' Spag said desperately. 'If he's really lost, Mum and Dad'll have to telegraph to Aunt Rachel and Uncle Gregory to come back, and there'll be a fearful row, and I'll never get my calculator, and – '

'Calm down.' Barny patted him on the arm. 'The trouble with you, Spag, is that you're very clever, but you can't think. It's no use running round in circles flapping. What we've got to do is go back to the place where he was last seen and look for clues.' He quite liked the idea. He had always known he could be a great detective. 'Now where was the last place?'

'Over there by Woolworth's.' Spag pointed across the road and looked as though he was about to run straight there, through the traffic. Clipper seized his collar and hauled him back.

'I'm not getting killed for anyone. And especially not for that little beast. We'll go through the subway.'

She marched off, round the end of the subway

57

and halfway down the slope which led into the tunnel. Then they saw her stop. Her mouth dropped open, and she gave a curious, choking splutter.

'What is it?' called Barny. But she could only splutter again and point into the subway. The others raced up to her and looked over her shoulder.

There, in the very middle of the subway, stood Denzil. He was wearing a dirty old beret that flopped over his forehead and a huge shirt of Spag's father's that billowed round him like an artist's smock. Across his top lip was a thin black line like a moustache, drawn in felt pen, and between his feet a large square of card was propped up.

Starving Artist it said.
Please give generously.

On the ground, on both sides of him, were long squiggles of the familiar bright green, which occupied about half the width of the subway.

A small group of people had gathered round. Most of them were shaking their heads and frowning. The only one who looked as though he were enjoying himself was the old man in the wheelchair they had seen on Denzil's first day at school. He was watching everyone with an amused grin and chuckling to himself.

Spag raced down the subway and caught Denzil by the scruff of his neck.

'What do you think you're doing?'

'Ouch! Let go!' Denzil struggled free. 'I'm being a pavement artist. To raise money for my Bat-mobile. And I'm brilliant. Look.' He pointed at the

60

squiggles all around him. 'That's Batman – me, I mean. And that's Robin. And that's the Batboat – '

'You're begging,' Spag shouted. 'And that's illegal.'

'I'm not begging. I'm – '

But before Denzil could say what he was doing, a cross-faced woman stepped out of the crowd and dug Spag in the ribs.

'Is this your little brother?'

'What?' Spag turned. 'Certainly not! He's my cousin.'

'Well, you ought to be ashamed of yourself.' The woman prodded him again. 'Letting him wander about on his own like that.'

'Yes.' Other people joined in. 'Poor little soul. Bound to get into mischief.'

All at once, everyone seemed to be talking and telling Spag that it was all his fault. He wriggled awkwardly.

'Let's get out of here,' he whispered to Barny and Clipper.

But before they could move, a voice from the far end of the subway said, 'Here he is, officer. Along here.'

They looked round. A fussy woman was walking towards them, hauling a large policeman after her.

'That's *all* we need,' muttered Spag. It was Soppy Mrs Potter, Elaine's mother.

Clipper acted first. She scooped up the piece of cardboard, crumpling it in her hands, and dragged her foot across the ground, smearing the toothpaste pictures into an unrecognisable mess.

61

'My pictures!' wailed Denzil.

'Hurry up, officer,' Mrs Potter was saying. As she stepped up to the crowd, she caught sight of Barny, Spag and Clipper and her lips pursed disapprovingly, as though she had stepped in something nasty.

'*You* three. I might have known you'd be mixed up in this.'

'Now then,' said the policeman. 'We can't have this. The whole subway's blocked. Suppose you good people move along and let me sort this out. Mmm?'

Instantly, people began to move away, until none of the crowd was left, except the old man in the wheelchair, who simply stayed by the wall, grinning and staring.

The policeman pulled out his notebook. 'Now then, you kids, what's going on?'

As usual, it was Barny who was ready with an explanation. 'It was an accident,' he said quickly. 'Denzil had an accident with a tube of toothpaste. It squelched all over the ground.'

The policeman looked at him suspiciously and then at the mess of green. Then he looked down at his notebook and the corners of his mouth twitched.

'According to my informant,' he looked sideways at Soppy Mrs Potter, as though he did not like her much, 'this little boy was drawing pictures with toothpaste and asking passers-by to give money for looking at them.'

Barny smiled confidently at him. 'But that's ridiculous. He wouldn't expect anyone to give him money for *his* pictures. They're terrible.'

Denzil opened his mouth to protest, but Clipper pinched his elbow.

'Look, I'll show you,' Barny said helpfully. 'Go on, Denzil. Draw a picture of Batman.'

Denzil did not need to be persuaded. Reaching under the gigantic shirt, he pulled another tube of toothpaste out of his trouser pocket, pulled off the cap and began to squirt a long, green trail on to the ground.

'There you are,' he said proudly. 'Batman. Isn't it brilliant?'

The policeman looked, speechless. Behind him, the old man in the wheelchair gave a squawk of laughter. Very slowly, the policeman walked round the picture in a small circle, staring down. Then he looked up at Barny.

'I see what you mean,' he said gravely. 'No one could expect to get money for that.'

Very slowly, Barny let out his breath in a silent sigh of relief. But he relaxed a bit too soon. The policeman was looking carefully at them all.

'All the same, we can't have this mess blocking up the subway. People'll be tracking it everywhere on their shoes. You'd better clean it up sharpish. I don't want to see a drop of toothpaste when I come back this way in half an hour. Otherwise, I'm sure this lady,' he gestured at Mrs Potter, 'will be able to tell me your names and addresses, and I'll be round to see your parents. So get cleaning.'

He strode away up the subway and Mrs Potter

followed him, twittering, 'Is that all you're going to do, officer?'

'Get that shirt off, Denzil,' Spag said sternly. 'We'll have to use it to mop up the toothpaste.'

'But it's my *smock*,' Denzil protested. 'I need it for being an artist and – '

He would have gone on arguing, but the old man in the wheelchair suddenly interrupted. 'Psst!'

Startled, they looked round, and the old man grinned. 'I said "Psst". Come over here, little lad.'

Denzil walked over, and the old man wriggled sideways in his chair, reaching into his pocket.

'Haven't had such a jolly Saturday morning in years. Reckon I owe you something for that. Here.' He pulled out a pound note and pressed it into Denzil's hand. 'You'll do all right, lad, when you latch on to something you're good at. But I should give the painting a miss. Wasting your time there, you are.'

'Th – thank you.' Even Denzil was taken aback. He looked down at the pound note and then back at the old man, as though he could not quite believe his luck.

'Right then,' snapped the old man, suddenly stern. 'Now, you get that shirt off and help your friends clean up that mess. Before I run you over with my wheelchair.'

'Y – yes,' stuttered Denzil.

The old man nodded briskly and propelled himself off up the subway as Denzil began to undo the buttons of the shirt.

'It's always the same,' grumbled Clipper as she

got down on to her knees. 'It all ends up with us having to clean something. If he doesn't go away soon, I'll get housemaid's knee.'

Barny looked superior. 'That's the trouble with you, Clipper. You're too skinny. If you were properly padded, like me, you'd be able to put up with it.'

Clipper did not say anything. Just took the shirt from Denzil and held it out to Barny.

5 · Enter Thrasher Dyson

'Oh no,' said Spag. '*Oh* no.' He glared at Barny and Clipper and tried to shut the door in their faces. But Clipper stuck her foot into the gap.

'Look, don't be dim. This isn't dangerous, even if it *is* one of Gobbo's ideas.'

'What do you mean?' Barny bristled. 'My ideas are brilliant.'

'Brilliant at getting us into trouble,' Spag said. 'I don't know how you have the cheek to turn up here with something else for Denzil to do. Not after last time.'

'But this is different,' wheedled Clipper. 'We don't want him to go off by himself. We just want to keep him busy so that you can help us pick the team for the semi-final on Saturday. We *need* you, Spag.' She saw him begin to waver and gave Barny a push. 'Go on, Gobbo. Show him.'

Barny held out the box. 'Look, it's a model kit. That's all. We'll sit him down at the table and tell

66

him to make up this ship. And while he's doing it, we can go through the records and pick the best team.' He looked craftily at Spag. 'When we've studied the statistics.'

Spag hesitated. 'Well – '

'I knew you'd see sense.' Clipper pushed past him into the hall. 'You don't want us to do it without you, do you?'

'Not that we couldn't,' Barny smirked. That made up Spag's mind. He reached out a long arm and pulled Barny into the house, slamming the door.

'Stow it, Gobbo. You couldn't work out a batting average in a hundred years.'

Barny glanced round. 'Where *is* the fiendish Denzil, then?'

'He's in the kitchen with Mum. Helping her make a cake.'

'I'll go and rescue her,' Barny said grandly. 'If she's really grateful, she might give us a bit of the cake later on.'

He made for the kitchen. Mrs Barlow was by the cooker, spreading mixture into a cake tin and looking harassed. Denzil was standing in the sink, lecturing her while he scooped golden syrup out of a tin with his fingers.

' – and my mother always puts glacé cherries in all her cakes.'

'Not in Swiss rolls, dear,' Mrs Barlow said feebly. 'Will you please get out of the sink?'

'Especially in Swiss rolls.' Denzil grabbed another handful of syrup and crammed most of it into

67

his mouth. The rest dribbled down his tee-shirt. 'She says I need a lot of sweet things to keep up my energy and – oh, hallo, Big Bum.'

Mrs Barlow looked round. 'Hallo, Barny.' Somehow, she did not sound overjoyed. She'll soon see, thought Barny. He nodded kindly at her and marched across to the sink.

'Come out of there, you. I've brought you something good to do. Come into the sitting-room.'

'Not like that!' wailed Mrs Barlow.

'OK, OK.' Grabbing a dishcloth, Barny held it under the cold tap. Not paying any attention to Denzil's protests, he rubbed at his face and hands and tee-shirt until they were damp but clean. Then he heaved him out of the sink and stood him on the floor.

'Come on, then. It's really good.'

Rather suspiciously, Denzil followed the three of them into the sitting-room and gave a wary look at the box which Barny put down on the table.

'What's that?'

'It's a ship that you make yourself,' Clipper said. 'You follow the instructions and glue it together.'

'Oh,' said Denzil.

'It's a destroyer,' put in Spag.

Denzil brightened. 'What does it destroy?'

'Oh, things.' Barny waved a hand vaguely. 'Want me to show you how to do it?'

'Course not.' Denzil sniffed. 'I'm brilliant at models. My mother says – '

'Your mother talks too much.' Fiercely, Clipper steered him towards the table and pushed him down into a chair. 'You just get that kit out and read the instructions. You can read, I suppose?'

'Course I can read. I'm the best reader in my class. My mother says – '

He caught Clipper's eye and fell silent. She watched him for a moment or two as he tipped the pieces out of the box and began to read the instruction leaflet. Then she crossed the room to join the others, stretching out on her stomach on the floor, with the scorebook in front of her and her legs waving in the air.

'Now look, what we're after – still – is more runs. We're not badly off for bowlers. There's me and Shane Denny and Laurie Symes. But we haven't got any reliable batsmen except Spotty McGrew and me – '

'I'm a brilliant batsman,' came a high-pitched voice from the other side of the room. 'My mother says – '

'Oh, shut up!' Clipper hurled the words over her shoulder and then turned back to the others. 'What we've got to do is check and check again. All the figures for this year and last year. To make sure we haven't forgotten anyone.'

Spag reached for a piece of paper, looking utterly gloomy. Really enjoying himself, thought Barny.

'What we need,' he muttered, 'is someone who can be relied upon to score twelve or fifteen. Not someone who *might* score twenty-five or thirty on a good day.'

'Twenty-five's a pathetic score,' chipped in

Denzil. 'I can score hundreds and hundreds and hundreds.'

They ignored him and plunged into a sea of figures, arguing loudly whenever Spag's sums squashed one of their good ideas. Finally, he put down his pen in disgust.

'Look, this is maths I'm doing, not magic, Clipper. There *isn't* anyone with an average of over ten, except you and Spotty.'

'Hey – ' came Denzil's voice. Clipper gnashed her teeth.

'I don't want to hear another sound out of you, pipsqueak! Understand? *Not another sound.*' She propped her chin on her hand. 'There's got to be *someone*, Spag. Let's go through it all again.'

Silently, she and Barny began to check down the list of names, while Spag watched with grim satisfaction. He did not need to check. His sums were always right.

While they were still brooding, Mrs Barlow came into the room. She jumped when she saw them.

'What are you all doing here?'

Spag looked round. 'We're working out the cricket team.'

'But Denzil said you were going down to the park to sail the boat he's made. He came into the kitchen to tell me, about ten minutes ago. And of course I said it was all right, if he was going with you.'

'What?' Spag jumped up and stared across at the table. But there was no Denzil. And no boat. Just a large pool of glue, rapidly drying in the middle of the polished surface.

Mrs Barlow sighed angrily. 'Honestly, James, I don't know why you can't take better care of him. He's only a little boy.'

'All right, all right.' Spag was already at the door. 'We'll find him. He can't have got far.'

'Don't worry, Mrs Barlow,' said Barny. 'We're getting to be experts at looking after Denzil. We'll keep him out of trouble, if anyone can.'

'*If* anyone can,' murmured Clipper, as she followed the other two out of the room.

Mrs Barlow sighed and began to clean the glue off the table.

They ran down the road towards the park without talking, all silent for different reasons. Spag was busy worrying about what Denzil might have got up to with ten minutes' lead. Clipper was sulking because her team selection had been interrupted. And Barny did not talk because he was panting too hard.

So they all heard the wails clearly. Loud sobs, coming from the direction of the park. Dashing through the gates, they saw a little girl of about four clutching something bright green to her chest as she raced towards them. There were long green smears down her dress and rubbed on to her cheeks, and as she got closer to them they could see that what she was carrying was a toy yacht, daubed with toothpaste.

'It sinked!' she howled. 'It sinked to the very bottom, and now it's horrid!'

They did not stop to ask her any questions. They

just ran across the park to the pond as fast as they could.

Denzil was standing right in the middle of it, with water up to his waist, facing the notice that said:

THIS IS **NOT** A PADDLING POOL.
PLEASE KEEP OUT OF THE WATER.

In one hand, he held the boat he had made, a strange jumble of grey plastic pieces, stuck together in any order. In the other, he gripped a large tube of toothpaste. 'I'm Batman,' he was shouting. 'And this is my Batdestroyer!'

Clipper pulled off her trainers and began to tug at her socks, but Barny laid a hand on her arm.

'That's the trouble with you, Clipper. You always rush in like a mad gorilla. Denzil needs *intelligent* handling.'

'You might as well go home, then,' jeered Clipper. But she slipped her feet back into her shoes and watched as Barny strode to the edge of the pond.

'I thought Batman was a crime-fighter,' he yelled across the water.

'That's right,' Denzil shouted back. 'I am. I kill super-criminals.'

Then he turned as a wooden boat came bobbing up to him. With a quick squelch, he squirted toothpaste all over it and, overwhelmed by the extra weight, the boat began to sink. At the edge of the pool, a little boy burst into tears.

'*He's* not a super-criminal,' Barny said.

'Course he is.' Denzil sounded scornful. 'They're

brilliant at disguises, you know. But I can see through them, because I'm Batman.'

He waved the toothpaste tube above his head and went on shouting. All the little children clustered round the pool began to snatch their precious boats out of the water and hurry away, pulling faces at Denzil over their shoulders. In a moment or two, he was all alone in the pond and he looked round blankly. Then, very slowly, he began to screw the cap back on to the tube of toothpaste.

'There,' whispered Barny cheerfully. 'Told you the intelligent way was best. He'll come out in a minute or two, when he sees there's no one left to annoy.'

'I hope he does,' muttered Spag, in an odd, strained voice. 'Look over there.'

A large, solid boy was marching over the grass towards the opposite edge of the pond. His bristly hair was cropped short on his head and he had a flat, ferocious face. Under his arm, he carried a big radio-controlled boat. As they watched, he knelt down on the kerb at the edge of the pond and began trying to start the engine.

Barny gulped. 'Denzil'll *have* to come out now.'

'He doesn't know about Thrasher Dyson,' Spag said quietly. 'He's never seen him.'

'But just the look of him – ' muttered Barny.

Thrasher caught sight of the three of them staring at him. He raised his head and grinned, baring large, dirty teeth.

'Well, well, if it isn't the freaks from the Bennett School. Lost any good cricket matches lately?'

74

'Why?' said Clipper. 'Frightened you might have to play us?'

Barny tugged at her arm to keep her quiet. 'Don't annoy him. We've got to get Denzil out of that pond.'

Thrasher picked up the last few words. 'Oh, he's yours, is he? Didn't know you'd taken up baby-minding. Looks as though you're almost as bad at that as you are at cricket.'

Denzil went red in the face. 'I'm not a baby!' he yelled. 'I'm Batman. And if you don't watch out, I'll KAPOW your boat with my Batdestroyer.'

'Oh yeah?' jeered Thrasher. 'You and who else?' He started the engine of his glossy red boat and it began to whine on a steady, high note as he dropped it into the water. 'Look, midget, no one threatens Thrasher, see? Not if they want to live.'

Picking up the control box, he began to move the switches so that the boat swooped round Denzil in large circles, sending ripples of water up his body.

'You watch out!' Denzil shouted. 'Or you'll be sorry.'

'Boo hoo,' grinned Thrasher. 'Coo, you scare me. You're so big and strong.' He moved the controls again and the large scarlet boat swung closer to Denzil, whizzing round in a long oval, so that it banged him as it passed. Chuckling, Thrasher made it swing round, ready to attack again.

Slowly, Denzil took the cap off his tube of tooth-paste.

'Oh – oh!' said Spag.

'Don't worry.' Barny tried to sound soothing. 'That boat's huge. Denzil couldn't sink it, even if he squeezed twenty tubes of toothpaste over it.'

'Yes,' said Spag. 'But ...'

He did not have time to explain. As the boat came at him again, banging his back, Denzil spun round and squirted, with perfect aim and perfect timing. The toothpaste landed neatly on the motor at the back of the boat. For a moment the motor went on running, whirling bright green shreds into the air and making choking noises. Then it stopped abruptly.

'Hmm,' said Clipper. 'Time for mad gorilla tactics.'

She plunged into the water, not bothering to take her shoes off this time, and seized Denzil by the scruff of his neck and the seat of his trousers. On the other side of the pond, Thrasher was bellowing with rage and peeling off his socks.

'Come on, sunshine,' said Clipper. 'This is where we *scoot*.' Ignoring Denzil's wails of protest, she hauled him to the bank and pushed him up out of the water, seizing him again as she vaulted out herself.

'Right now. *Run*.'

Loud splashing noises were coming from the pond as Thrasher waded into the water, picked up his boat and carried on towards them. He was grinding his teeth and growling. Then he began to snort through his nose.

'Coo!' panted Clipper as she and Spag pulled Denzil towards the gates. 'He's getting really wild. I could have a lovely punch-up with him now.'

'Don't you dare!' Barny forced the words out, even though it hurt him to speak while he was running. 'If you – fight in the – park – your mum'll stop you – playing cricket – punishment.'

'I know.' Clipper groaned as she tugged at Denzil to try and make him run faster.

Without needing to discuss it, they made straight for Barny's house, because it was the nearest. And they were only just in time. Darting through the big, wooden gates which said J. F. GOBBO. SECONDHAND FURNITURE. HOUSES CLEARED, they crashed them together and slid the bolt across. Then they ducked behind a huge rusty water tank as Thrasher thudded against the barrier. They did not think he would be put off by something as feeble as a bolted gate.

And he wasn't. He seized the gates and began to rattle them backwards and forwards, jarring the ancient hinges and chanting terrible threats. Behind the water tank, they held their breath.

Then another voice sounded, from the kitchen window. A voice even louder than Thrasher's.

'Barny Gobbo! Is that you, you little wretch?'

Automatically, Barny opened his mouth to say no. Then he shut it again. This could be interesting.

Thrasher shook the gates and roared again.

'Do I have to come out there and *make* you stop?' Mrs Gobbo roared back. 'You'll be sorry if I do, my lad!'

Paying no attention, Thrasher banged harder at

77

the gates and let out a stream of such awful language that even Denzil blinked.

Mrs Gobbo erupted through the kitchen door and into the yard, and Denzil gaped, because he had never seen her before. It was not just that there was a lot of her, although there certainly was. What made her bulk really terrifying was that she looked ready to throw it at anyone who stepped out of line.

She rushed straight across the yard, slid the bolt back and flung the gates open so suddenly that Thrasher nearly fell at her feet.

'Yes?' she barked.

He looked at her.

'You wanted something?'

He shook his head meekly.

'Well, next time you fancy making a noise like that, go and bang your head on the middle of the road.'

'Y - yes,' muttered Thrasher, as though he thought it would be nicer than facing Mrs Gobbo. Without another word, he slid away up the road.

Mrs Gobbo waited until the sound of his feet died in the distance. Then she said, quite softly for her, 'And if you imagine I don't know you're behind that water tank, Barny Gobbo, you must think my brain's rotted. *Which* it hasn't. So you'd better not dare come inside until you've thought of something good to say for yourself.'

She stamped off, back to the kitchen.

'Cripes,' said Barny.

'Not your fault,' Spag muttered. 'She won't be angry if you tell her everything, will she?'

'Won't she?' Barny looked doubtful.

'Tell her it's all Batman's fault.' Clipper looked severely at Denzil. 'I hope you're grateful, boot-face. I reckon I saved your life.'

Denzil stood up. 'No, you didn't!' he shrilled, stamping his foot. 'You just stopped me when I was having fun. You're always the same. A rotten spoil-sport, Clipper Young. Just you wait till I tell my mother you've been stunting my development and stopping me expressing myself.'

He raced off through the gate, and Clipper stared after him.

'I wish *I* could express myself. I know *just* what I'd do!'

6 · Clipper's Bat

Barny went slowly through the kitchen door. He had put it off as long as he could, hanging about outside with the others, but they had had to go at last. And now he had to go in and face his mother.

She was sitting at the kitchen table, preparing apples for a pie. The long twists of green peel curled over her muscular wrists to fall on the table. She did not stop when he came in. Did not even look up. Just snapped, 'Well?'

'It wasn't my fault,' Barny said quickly. 'I haven't done anything wrong.'

'Expect me to believe that?' His mother frowned up at him. 'It was that Thrasher Dyson from King's Road, wasn't it? I suppose he was chasing you for nothing. Bit of fun and games, eh? I'm not daft, you know. You've done something to get up his nose, and if you've got any sense, you'll tell me now.'

'It wasn't *me*. It was Spag's cousin Denzil. He – '

'Barny Gobbo! If you're in trouble, you just stand up and face it! Don't you go blaming it on someone else.' She waved the apple in her hand as though she wanted to throw it at him. Then something in his face must have changed her mind, because she put the apple down and peered more closely at him. 'You scared, then? Frightened of that Thrasher?'

Barny slumped down into a chair and rubbed his nose. 'It's not just him. It's everything. It seems to be getting out of hand. Denzil – ' He stopped and looked up at her, but she did not shout at him this time. Just tossed him a piece of apple peel to eat and signalled to him to go on.

So Barny told her. He told her all the things that had happened ever since Denzil arrived. For the first few minutes, she grinned, enjoying the joke of it, but by the time he had finished, her face was completely serious.

'Poor little bleeder,' she said softly.

'Oh, it's not that bad.' Barny was surprised. 'I'm not *really* scared. Honest.'

'Not you, lunk-head. You're OK. Tough as old boots. No, it's that poor little Denzil I'm sorry for. Sounds like he's been messed about all his life. Doesn't do a kid any good to have his mum making him out a genius. Catch me doing that.'

'But I *am* a genius,' Barny said, injured.

His mother barely heard him. She put the peeled apple down on the table and chopped it fiercely into small pieces. 'And that Spag's been told to look after him?' She snorted. 'Couldn't look after a goldfish! Got nothing in his head but arithmetic.'

'Spag's all right,' Barny said loyally. 'He's just – '

'Just not the right person to look after a little tearaway like that Denzil,' his mother finished for him. 'Be different if it was Clipper.' Her face softened. She liked Clipper.

'Clipper's no good,' Barny said. 'She can't think about anything except winning this cricket competition. She's mad enough with Denzil already, because he's stopping Spag joining in with that. Poor old Spag. He hasn't been able to score at all, yet, and it's the semi-final next Saturday.'

Mrs Gobbo nodded and started to peel the last apple. 'I'll think a bit. Give us a little while. I reckon that Spag deserves a day off.'

'Oh, Mum,' said Barny, 'it'd be super if you could think of a way.'

'That's enough, now.' Mrs Gobbo chopped the apple and stood up to fetch the flour for the pastry. 'Now, you get out of here. Can't stand having people in my hair when I'm cooking.'

'Yes, Mum, and – '

'OUT!' she shouted.

'Only wanted to say thanks,' muttered Barny as he made for the door.

'SPAG!' Clipper said joyfully. She tossed the cricket ball into the air and caught it neatly. 'What are you doing here?'

'Come to score for the semi-final,' said Spag,

quite calm. He sat down on the grass and pulled a packet of felt pens out of his pocket. 'If you want me to.'

Clipper looked suspiciously at him. 'Depends. Is Batman going to come sneaking up on us any moment?'

Spag grinned. 'Nope.'

'But how – ?'

'It was Gobbo's mum,' Spag said. 'She was fantastic. She turned up at our house just now, out of the blue, and said she was going to borrow Denzil for the afternoon. She'd looked out your old two-wheeler, Gobbo, and she's going to teach him to ride it.'

'Oh, I do love your mum, Gobbo!' Clipper shrieked. 'She's really great.'

'Oh, I just had a word with her,' Barny said, hiding his surprise. 'Told her to think of something.'

Clipper was already springing into action. 'Look, Spag, we're fielding first, so grab one of those St Crispin's kids and get their batting order out of him. I'm going to open the bowling, with Laurie Symes. But if we haven't got a wicket in the first five overs, I'll swap him for Shane Denny.' She swung her arms vigorously, like a windmill. 'But I reckon we'll have them all out in a quarter of an hour. I feel like shattering the stumps today.'

But it wasn't as easy as that. The St Crispin's team looked meek and mild. Most of them were short and they behaved very quietly and politely. But they had been taught by a keen, careful teacher

84

and they did not go weak at the knees when Clipper thundered down the pitch towards them. Instead, they played cautiously, blocking her wilder balls and hitting the slower ones all round the field. Laurie Symes and Shane Denny were treated even worse and, when the St Crispin's innings closed at the end of twenty-five overs, they had scored eighty and lost only five wickets.

'Should be all over soon,' their captain yelled cheerfully to Clipper as the Bennett team came off the field. 'We've heard all about your batting.'

As Clipper came up the slope towards Spag, she buried her face in her hands.

'Five wickets!' she groaned. 'We didn't even get them all out! It's disastrous. And now they've got so many runs, they're bound to be cocky.'

Barny slouched over and began to unfasten his wicket-keeper's pads. 'Don't be such a wet blanket, Clipper. We've got twenty-five overs. We'll get the runs.'

'Oh, we've got lots of overs.' Clipper scowled at him. 'It's not *overs* we're short of.'

Spag whistled a little tune through his teeth as he wrote down the names of the Bennett School batsmen. 'Glad I'm not playing, Clipper. I wouldn't fancy getting bashed round the ribs with your bat when I was out.'

'Oh, I wouldn't bash you with my *bat*.' Clipper sounded shocked. 'Not after all the trouble I had getting Mum to buy me a new one. I might damage it. No,' she grinned suddenly, 'I'd use an iron bar.'

Spotty McGrew came sprinting across, the tops

of his pads flapping. 'Come on, Clip. Stop wasting time. Thought you were going to open with me today.'

Clipper shook herself and reached for a pair of pads. As she started to buckle them, Soppy Elaine and Sharon Grove came prinking up the road and peered through the fence at her.

'Are you winning?' said Soppy Elaine.

'Go away,' growled Clipper.

'But I came *specially* to watch. Didn't we, Sharon?' Soppy Elaine giggled. 'Those St Crispin's boys are so nice and polite.'

'Come on, Spotty.' Clipper stood up. 'I think it's healthier out on the wicket than it is here.' And she clumped off down the slope.

Twenty minutes later, she was back, her shoulders slouching and her bat trailed behind her. 'Ten!' she muttered. 'Ten, and a lousy total of twenty. And we've had nearly half the overs.' She made to swipe the ground with her bat and then remembered and kicked the grass instead. 'We'll be slaughtered.'

'Ah!' said Soppy Elaine, in tones of deep sympathy. 'And I thought you were so *good*, Clipper.'

Barny stuck his tongue out at her. 'Don't be soft,' he said to Clipper. 'We can still do it. Don't forget – I haven't batted yet.'

Clipper snorted. 'Oh, that will make *all* the difference.' Spag looked across and grinned sarcastically.

Despite Barny's rage, they were right. He had hardly started his innings before he was trailing

86

back in his turn. He had scored only one run and they still had twenty-five to make in five overs. True, Spotty McGrew was still there, but there was only one wicket left to fall and Jimmy Brown, walking out to bat, looked very small and scared.

'Huh!' Clipper said bitterly, as if she were choking, 'it'll be all over in five minutes.' But she remembered her duty as captain, and waved cheerfully to encourage Jimmy Brown as he took guard.

Then, before the St Crispin's bowler could begin his run-up, there was a most appalling noise in the road outside the park. Yelling and screaming in three different voices. Barny, Spag and Clipper whirled round and saw an incredible chase coming up the road.

In front was Denzil, riding a shiny racing bicycle about three sizes too big for him. Most of the time he had to stand up on the pedals, gripping the handlebars tightly. But every now and again he sat down, stuck out a hand behind him and squirted toothpaste all over the road. He was shouting, 'Yah! Can't catch me! I'm Batman on my Batbike!'

Behind, red in the face and ferocious, was Thrasher Dyson, riding Barny's old two-wheeler, which was much too small for him. Every time he turned the pedals, he hit himself on the chin with his knees. He was bellowing, 'I'll get you, you thieving little monster!' He looked even worse than usual, because Barny's old bike had lost its mudguards and the front wheel was throwing toothpaste up all over his face and clothes.

Last of all, rapidly losing ground but pushing

dementedly, was the old man in the wheelchair. He was yelling, 'Why don't you chase someone your own size, you great bully?'

'I might have known it was too good to last,' muttered Spag. He put the scorebook down. 'I'll have to – '

'Sit down.' Clipper squashed him firmly down, with a hand on each shoulder. 'You can't go. You're scoring.'

'But I can't let – '

'We'll do it.' Clipper rubbed her hands together. 'I shall enjoy splatting that rotten Denzil. Come on, Gobbo.'

Without waiting for him, she was away. Spag settled down with a sigh and signalled to the bowler that he was ready to score.

Barny panted after Clipper. She was making for the gate at the far end of the park, to cut off the cyclists as they came round the bend in the road. Her legs pumped at top speed and, as she whisked through the gate, she launched herself at the bicycles without any regard for her bones.

Denzil crashed to the ground and Thrasher thudded into the back of him.

'Right!' Huge and menacing, Thrasher untangled himself from the two machines.

Clipper scrambled up and faced him firmly. 'What do you mean "Right", you great bully?'

Thrasher stuck out his bottom jaw and glared at her. 'I mean right I'm going to scrag that little monster, that's what. He stole my bike and squirted me with toothpaste.'

88

'It's all your fault,' Denzil said coolly. 'You waited till Big Bum's mother was on the phone and then you came and laughed at me and snatched my bike away. So I took yours. Fair's fair.'

Clipper shook him to make him be quiet. Then she turned back to Thrasher. 'You can't scrag him, because I'm going to. He's interfered with everything ever since he came, and now he's loused up my cricket match. I get first scrag.'

'We could both scrag him together,' Thrasher said hopefully.

At that moment, the old man in the wheelchair caught up with them. 'You great bully,' he croaked at Thrasher. 'Why don't you leave the little boy alone?'

'He started it,' Thrasher said sulkily.

'*You* started it!' shrieked Denzil.

'Don't care who started it,' the old man said firmly. 'Big boys shouldn't get at little ones. That's all I know. Now get off home, you, or I'll be round to see your mother.'

Thrasher untangled his bike and glared at Denzil. 'You wait – *Batman*!' he muttered. 'You'll see me again.'

He clambered on to his bike and pedalled away, and Clipper turned to the old man. 'Thanks, Mr – er – ' she said. 'It was good you came up then. Saved me a lot of bother.'

The old man chuckled. 'You didn't look as though you needed any help. I like to see a girl who can take care of herself.' He jabbed a finger towards Denzil. 'Just keep an eye on that young monkey.

Needs to *do* something, he does. He's like a loose end, waiting for something to tie up.'

'Pity he can't tie himself up,' Clipper said crossly. She seized Denzil's ear and began to drag him into the park. 'Bring the bike, Gobbo.'

Pushing the bike along behind, Barny could hear Denzil muttering, 'You've done it again! Stopped me when I was having fun. I'll get my own back on you, Clipper.'

Clipper hauled him up the park, past all the players, who were strolling off the pitch, and flung him down on the grass beside Spag. 'What do you mean, you'll get me? *I'll* get *you*. You've made me miss the end of the cricket match. It looks really bad for the captain to walk off when her team's being beaten. They'll think I was sulking.'

Lazily, Spag closed the scorebook and looked up at her. 'You are dumb, Clipper.'

'Dumb!' Clipper nearly jumped on him. 'Is that all you can say after I've risked life and limb to save your wretched cousin?'

'We've won.'

'Wha-at?'

Spag smiled. 'We've won. We're in the final.'

For a moment, Clipper was speechless.

Spag nodded. 'Jimmy managed to stay in, and Spotty made forty-one.'

'Yaroo!' shrieked Clipper. She raced off down the slope to clap Spotty on the back.

'So we've still got a chance of winning the cricket pitch,' murmured Barny.

'*If* we can find anyone to stand up to Thrasher's

bowling,' Spag reminded him. 'We only won by a fluke today. That's not going to happen again.'

But Clipper was already working on that one. As she came back up with Spotty, her face was set stubbornly, and she was talking at top speed.

' – we *can't* let ourselves be beaten. Not now. I'll get everyone down here after school on Wednesday for batting practice and – '

Suddenly she broke off, looked round and pulled a face at Barny. 'OK, Gobbo. Where is it? What have you done with it?'

'Me?' said Barny. 'What? Where? Why? Whatever it was, I didn't do it.'

'Don't fool about,' Clipper said wearily. 'What have you done with my bat?'

'Ooh!' said Soppy Elaine. 'Was that *your* bat?'

They had forgotten she was there. Glancing round at her, they saw that she was smirking cheerfully.

'I thought it was *his* bat,' she trilled. 'The way he snatched it up.'

Clipper looked down at the ground and counted to three. Then she said, 'Elaine, it was my best bat. Where was who taking it?'

'He went off with Jimmy Brown,' Elaine said airily. 'Said he'd play cricket with him up behind the cemetery.'

Clipper seized the railings in her fists and rattled them. '*Who?*'

Elaine raised her eyebrows. 'Goodness, what a fuss about an old cricket bat! Anyway, it was only Denzil. Come on, Sharon. We'll be late for tea.'

Clipper stood quite still for a moment, unable to move or speak. Then she said, as if she were strangling, 'If he's damaged it, I'll – I'll – '

Barny looked at her anxiously. 'Calm down a bit, Clipper. I don't think you ought to – I mean, he *is* Spag's cousin.'

'Yes, she ought,' Spag said miserably. 'He's the worst cousin anyone ever had, but even *he* ought to have known not to touch Clipper's bat. Come on. Let's go and get it back.'

'It's probably too late,' Clipper said, with deathly calm. 'You know what Denzil's like. Still, we'd better try.'

She set off towards the cemetery, followed by the other two. For most of the way she walked, whistling casually, as though she did not particularly care. Behind her back, Spag and Barny looked nervously at each other.

Finally they reached the tall gates at the front of the cemetery. A high wall ran round the whole plot and, at the back, behind the far wall, was an open piece of waste ground that children played on. Now, as they stood at the gates, they could hear, coming from that direction, the sound of someone hitting a cricket ball.

It was too much for Clipper. With a sharp cry, she ran through the gates and past the graves, ignoring the frowns of people who were walking there. Barny and Spag hurried after her at a more respectable pace.

'Got to calm her down,' panted Barny. 'She'll kill him if he's damaged it.'

93

'Serve the little beast right,' growled Spag.

As they drew near the small gate in the far wall, they saw that Clipper had stopped. She was peering through the gate as though she wanted to stay hidden.

'Oh!' she whispered, in a voice of longing, 'oh, the little *fiend*!'

As she glanced back at them, they could see that her expression had changed completely.

7 · Plotting

Barny and Spag raced to look over her shoulder. Denzil was standing further along the wall, with his back to it, and Jimmy Brown was bowling at him. Casually, Denzil knocked the ball back, alternately to the right and to the left, so that Jimmy scampered wildly from one side to the other.

'Not bad,' said Barny tolerantly after a few moments. 'He hasn't missed one yet, has he?'

'Hasn't *missed* one?' Spag stared at him. 'Gobbo, you're loony. He's not just hitting them. He's playing lovely strokes.' Spag could not hit a ball himself, even if it was trickling along the ground, but he could recognise every shot in the book. He turned to Clipper. 'Go on, don't be too hard on him. The kid's good. You'll have to let him off.'

'Let him off?' Clipper said in a strange voice. 'I'm not going to let him off a thing. I'm going to give him a proper work-over.'

She stepped through the gate and strode towards

95

Jimmy, her face solemn. 'I'll have that ball.' She held out her hand for it. Then she turned to face Denzil. 'Don't *move*, Batman. You just stay there while we see how you face a real ball.'

Walking away from him, she turned and then came thundering forwards, her face set. Barny gasped in protest as he saw that she was about to bowl one of her really fast balls. Denzil was watching her with a cheeky grin, not looking in the least frightened.

As she loosed the ball, he stepped forward and played confidently, driving it back along the ground, so straight that it almost grazed her ankles as she finished running.

'Wow!' said Spag.

Clipper did not give any sign of pleasure. She just waved a hand to tell Jimmy to fetch the ball and called to the others. 'Gobbo! Spag! Come out here and field. Then I can give Denzil a real belting.'

For the next half hour they worked hard, until Barny was red-faced and panting, and Spag's glasses were slithering down his sweaty nose. There was hardly any talking. Occasionally, Clipper would call out, 'Try and hook this one to leg' or 'See if you can drive this between Spag and Jimmy.'

Each time, Denzil did exactly what she had asked. His cheeky grin had gone and his peaky freckled face was completely solemn as he concentrated on the ball.

Finally Clipper stopped, out of breath, and ran towards the wall with a broad grin on her face.

'You're not bad at all, young Denzil,' she said.

'I'm brilliant. I told you I was.'

'Not like *that*.' Clipper gave an impatient stamp. 'You say you're brilliant at everything, even if you're lousy. But you really can bat.'

For a moment Denzil looked pleased and startled. Then his face switched back to its usual sulky expression. 'So?'

'So I'm putting you in the team.' Clipper smiled at him. 'You're just what we need to batter King's Road in the final. I'll even let you use my bat, if you like.'

For two blinks, Denzil stared at her without speaking. Then, very deliberately, he dropped the bat on the grass. 'I don't want to borrow your precious bat. And I don't want to be in your rotten team. You're a horrible, bossy girl, Clipper Young. Every time I've started to have fun, you've interfered and stopped me. Why should I help you out?'

'But – ' said Clipper.

Denzil started to walk away. 'I hope you lose,' he called over his shoulder. 'I hope they get you all out for three. That'll teach you to get in the way of Batman!'

'He's a copper-bottomed, four-flushing demon!' Clipper said bitterly. She trailed her bare toes in the goldfish pond and did not even smile when the goldfish came up to nibble them. 'What are we going to do?'

'You can see his point,' Spag murmured reasonably. 'You've done everything you could to keep

97

him out of the cricket up till now. I expect he wants to get his own back.'

Clipper ruffled her hands through her hair. 'But if he'd only *told* me.'

'He did tell you,' said Barny. 'Over and over again. You just wouldn't listen.'

'I know, I know, but – oh, blow it all, I've got to have him. It's not just winning the cricket pitch. It's such a *waste* if he doesn't bat when he's so good.'

'Well, if he won't, he won't.' Spag looked resigned. 'We can't make him.'

We could drag him along to the match,' suggested Barny. 'And sit on him until it was time for him to bat.'

The other two looked at him scornfully.

'Oh, sure,' said Spag. 'He'd just stand there and let Thrasher bowl him out. You know how stubborn he is. He won't do anything to oblige anyone else.'

The three of them stared gloomily down into the pond. They were so deep in their thoughts that they did not see Clipper's mother coming over the grass. They did not look up until her shadow fell across them. She was carrying a tray with three strawberry milkshakes in tall glasses and she gazed down at them with a puzzled expression.

'What's up with you three, then? Thought you'd all fancy milkshakes with ice-cream in.'

'Oh yes,' Barny said sadly. 'Thanks a million, Mrs Young.'

'Thanks, Mum.' Clipper took a glass and stared at it with dull eyes. 'Just what we wanted.'

98

Mrs Young narrowed her eyes and then sat down on the grass, tucking her legs underneath her. 'Suppose you tell me what's the matter. You look as though the sky's fallen in.'

'It's worse than that,' groaned Clipper. 'Much worse.' She drooped her head and sucked noisily at her straw.

Barny decided that he had better explain. The other two were useless. 'It's Spag's cousin Denzil – ' he began. Mrs Young gave a wide grin.

'Been up to his tricks again, has he? What is it this time? Worse than painting the subway with toothpaste?'

'Much worse.' Clipper groaned again.

'He's a brilliant batsman,' Spag explained in a mournful voice. 'A natural. We've only just discovered.'

'And that's not good?' Mrs Young looked bewildered. 'I thought you were desperate for batsmen.'

'It *could* be good,' Clipper muttered. 'It could be the best thing since England won the World Cup. Only he won't play. When I told him he was in the team for the final, he said he wouldn't do it. Just to annoy me.'

'You – told him?' Mrs Young said slowly. 'That's just like you, Caroline. I suppose you never thought to *ask*, instead?'

Clipper looked up in surprise and then hung her head, pulling at the grass. 'Never thought he wouldn't be pleased,' she mumbled. 'And all the little kids always do what I tell them.'

99

'Well, I'm glad Denzil didn't, then.' Her mother sounded severe. 'Like I'm always telling you, you're getting to be too bossy. Time you gave some thought to other people's feelings. You ought to go to him and ask politely.'

The three of them looked at her in horror.

'But we *can't*,' whispered Clipper. 'Not go to him and beg. Think how he'd gloat.'

'Besides,' Spag said, considering it, 'it wouldn't do any good. He'd say no again, just to annoy us.'

Mrs Young shrugged and stood up. 'If he's really like that, there's nothing you can do. Sounds like he won't play at all, unless *he* wants to.'

She walked away across the grass and Clipper dug her fingers into the earth and fumed. 'But he *ought* to want to. He would, if he weren't so dumb. It would let him have a go at Thrasher.'

Spag shook his head. 'I don't suppose he even knows Thrasher's in the King's Road team. How could he?'

Suddenly, Barny sat up and a huge smile spread over his face. 'I've got an Idea,' he announced.

'That's *all* we need,' Clipper exploded.

'Bliss, perfect bliss,' muttered Spag.

The two of them flung themselves at him, knocking him over and rubbing his face in the grass while they tickled him, until he was spluttering with rage.

'No, *listen*,' he said, as they let him go. 'It's brilliant. Really foolproof.' He lay back on the grass with his hands behind his head and looked up at the little clouds floating across the sky. 'This is what we've got to do.' And he began to explain.

By the time he had finished, the others were looking at him quite seriously and Clipper had even started to smile.

'You know,' she murmured, 'I think it just might work.'

'Right,' said Spag, as they came out on to the roof at breaktime on Monday, 'now don't be too obvious. Just look as though we're plotting, so that we catch her attention.'

They sneaked elaborately across the playground, glancing all round as if to make sure they were not being watched. Halfway, Spag dug Barny in the ribs.

'It's working, Gobbo. She's looking round at us. Now just give her a second to get here.'

The three of them ducked down into their private corner behind the chimneystacks and Clipper pressed her hand over her mouth to stop herself laughing. After a moment, they heard quick, light footsteps come tiptoeing over and stop suddenly. Spag nodded to Clipper.

'It's a secret,' she said, just loudly enough to carry to the other side of the chimneystacks. 'No one must know.'

There was the sound of another step and Barny smirked as he saw a familiar pigtailed shadow thrown against the wall at the edge of the playground.

'Especially Soppy Elaine,' he said. 'She's sure to tell. She'd probably tell Thrasher Dyson. He lives up her way, and she's always gabbing on to him.'

Clipper grinned broadly. 'Not *Thrasher*. He's the last person we want finding out. So you'll have to help us, Spag. We must all go round and tell the people in the team that there's a secret cricket practice in the park straight after school on Wednesday. We're going to work out our plan to deal with King's Road in the final.'

'Ah.' Spag nodded solemnly. 'I can see why you don't want Thrasher Dyson to know. He'd be really pleased to spy on what we were up to.'

'Yes,' said Barny. 'So remember. Warn all the kids it's a total, utter secret.'

'*Especially* from Soppy Elaine, tell them,' put in Clipper. 'You know what a blabbermouth she is.'

There was a short, stifled gasp from the other side of the chimneys and then the sound of feet hurrying away. Helpless with glee, Clipper hugged herself and writhed on the ground in silent laughter.

Barny peered round the chimneys to make sure they were alone again. 'That's all right, then. She'll never be able to resist passing on that piece of news. Everything should work perfectly as long as you can get Denzil down to the park on Wednesday, Spag. Think you can?'

Spag looked heroic. 'I'll tell him he can play with my radio-controlled aeroplane. He's bound to say yes to that. I just hope the plan works quickly. Before he has time to do anything awful to it.'

Barny felt a bit nervous as he trailed down to the park with the rest of the team on Wednesday. He knew his plan was a good one, but there were things that could go wrong with it. Suppose Denzil guessed what they were up to? Or Thrasher had to go to the dentist's? Barny chewed at the sides of his fingers.

By the time the stumps had been stuck in the ground, Spag and Denzil had appeared on the far side of the park. Denzil was crouched over the aeroplane, starting the engine, and Spag was fluttering anxiously round him, waiting for him to break the propeller.

Clipper ignored them and thumbed her nose absently at Soppy Elaine and Sharon Grove, who had tagged along as usual, so that they could make stupid remarks.

'Over here, everyone,' she called. When the cricketers were gathered round her in a tight little group, she began to whisper very softly. 'Now listen, everyone. I'm going to ask you to do something really weird. I can't explain for the moment, but you'll see why later on. I'm going to put each of you in to bat in turn and I want you all to be *terrible*. I don't care how you do it, but make yourselves look as though you'd never touched a cricket bat before. No matter how much I shout at you and call you names.' She gazed round at their puzzled faces and added, with heavy emphasis, '*Especially* if you see Thrasher Dyson.'

'That's not fair,' protested Spotty McGrew. 'Think I'm going to make an idiot of myself in front of Thrasher? It'll be all over King's Road by tomorrow morning.'

'Exactly.' Clipper winked at him and laid a finger along the side of her nose. 'We're being crafty.'

Spotty looked at her suspiciously and then shrugged. 'OK. You're the boss. I'll pretend I'm Soppy Elaine.'

He picked up his bat and minced out into the middle of the park, banging the ground in front of his stumps with coy little shrieks. Then he took guard, with his knees together and his feet apart.

'Don't overdo it,' said Clipper, trying not to giggle as she sent everyone else out to field.

Spotty enjoyed himself for five minutes or so, seeing how many different ways he could get out.

Each time, he squealed, 'Ooh, you are *rotten!*' in a squeaky imitation of Soppy Elaine's voice. And she knew what he was doing. Barny could see her sniffing and tossing her plaits.

But there was still no sign of Thrasher. Barny began to get worried. Surely Elaine couldn't have *kept* a secret? Not just when they wanted her to be her usual sneaking self. If Thrasher didn't come, the whole performance was useless. Denzil was looking scornful as batsman after batsman hit a catch or missed the ball completely, but he showed no signs of wanting to bat. Thrasher *had* to come.

Barny was so busy brooding that he missed a simple catch behind the wicket and Clipper yelled at him.

'You're a frightful wicket-keeper, Gobbo. You'd better come and bat instead. You can't do worse than this load of idiots.'

Just at that moment, Barny saw Soppy Elaine nudge Sharon Grove and snigger. Following her eyes, he made out a square, solid figure lurking behind the bushes at the bottom of the park. Feeling relieved, he took the bat from Jimmy Brown and turned to face Clipper's bowling.

'Watch out, everyone,' came a voice from the bushes. 'That's not the ball. It's Gobbo.'

Cheek! Barny went red with rage. He'd show that Thrasher. Just one lovely, Ian Botham shot, and then he would play as badly as Clipper wanted.

She sent him an easy ball and he swung his bat in a mighty curve, as hard as he could.

He missed the ball completely. It thudded into the stumps, knocking them out of the ground, while Barny fell over in an untidy heap.

'Gobbo!' yelled Clipper, sounding furious. 'You're worse than all the others.'

In a rage that was not quite pretended, Barny flung down his bat and stamped off towards the corner where Denzil and Spag were flying the aeroplane. Thrasher, watching him, suddenly caught sight of Denzil and jumped out from behind the bushes, purple in the face.

'Yah! You little rat,' he bellowed. 'You must be worse than all the others. Fancy being too bad to play in the *Bennett* team.'

'They'd like to have me,' Denzil shouted cheerfully. 'I'm brilliant.'

'Ha, ha. What's stopping you playing then? Don't you fancy facing my bowling? Always knew you were a little coward.'

Denzil stared at him for a moment and then handed the controls to Spag. '*Your* bowling?'

'Yeah. I'm the star King's Road bowler. None of this lot will be able to stand up to me. And you'd be worse, you little shrimp. You're not even good enough to play.'

Denzil hesitated. Then he looked across at Clipper. 'OK if I have a bat?' he shouted.

'Oh – all right. If you must.' Clipper tried to sound sulky and, behind Denzil's back, Spag winked at Barny.

'It's going even better than we hoped,' he whispered. 'Once he's shown how good he is, he'll *have*

106

to play. Or Thrasher will go round telling everyone he's scared.'

Rather slowly, Denzil took guard and nodded to Clipper that he was ready. As she came racing towards him, he lifted his bat and played.

He missed completely. The ball hit the wicket with a crack, knocking out the middle stump.

'Oh,' said Clipper in a strange voice, as Thrasher chortled. 'You'd better have another go.'

Denzil hit the second ball with the edge of the bat, so that it chipped backwards on to the wicket and sent the bails flying. Clipper frowned.

'This is your last chance,' she said, looking puzzled. When she ran up, she lacked her usual bounce, and the ball was slower than usual.

Denzil hit it square on. Right up into the air. It rose and rose and then dropped lazily down straight over Clipper's head, so that she had to catch it, in self defence.

'Thanks,' Thrasher called sarcastically. 'Thanks a lot. I can see we need to be *really* worried on Saturday.' Laughing loudly, he swaggered away down the road.

Barny, Spag and Clipper all made for Denzil, who was leaning on his bat, with a faint smile on his lips.

'And just what was *that* all about?' Clipper said icily.

Denzil smiled at her. A beautiful, beaming smile. 'I didn't want them to be warned about my batting, did I? Not if I'm going to play on Saturday.'

'You what?' Clipper gulped.

'Well, I've got to play, haven't I? If *he's* in their team. I'll knock his bowling all over the field.'

'Hang on a minute.' Clipper held up her hand severely. 'We don't want you playing if you're just going to show off. And you did say no before.'

'That's right,' said Barny. 'And no one's asked you again.'

The confident smile vanished from Denzil's face. 'But I do *want* to play.'

Spag grinned. 'Perhaps if you ask Clipper nicely, she might give in.'

Denzil blinked. Then he said, 'Please will you put me in the team for Saturday, Clipper?' She went on frowning at him and he looked anxious. 'I mean – I'm good. Well, quite good. Aren't I?'

'You're not bad,' Clipper said casually. 'All right, you can play. If you promise to behave yourself until then and do everything I ask you to. Right?'

'Right, Clipper,' Denzil said meekly.

8 · The Final

'Fuss!' said Clipper in disgust. She sat in the minibus with her bat between her knees and stared crossly out of the window. 'Just because it's the final, we've got to be introduced to the great Mr Grimes and say please and thank you and have a tea party afterwards. It's enough to make anyone nervous. Why can't we just get on with the game?'

'I think it's nice,' Barny protested. He wriggled in the narrow seat, squashing Spag, who was beside him. 'At least we'll get to play on Mr Grimes's cricket pitch, even if we don't win it.'

'What do you mean *even if we don't win*?' Clipper looked fierce. 'Of course we're going to win.' She glanced anxiously at Denzil, who was sitting next to her. 'We've got to win, haven't we, Spag?'

Spag frowned. 'I don't know that I can make a reliable prediction. I haven't studied the form of the King's Road team.'

'Oh, shut up!' Clipper poked him in the back of

the neck. 'We don't want sums. We want encouragement. Of course we're going to win. But I wish we didn't have to put up with all this grand stuff first.'

The minibus had turned up a long drive. Ahead of them was a big house and, to its left, the ground sloped down gently. At the foot of the slope was the cricket pitch, green and smooth, with a square of paler green marking the wicket. Clipper clutched her cricket bat tighter.

'Oh, it's a beautiful pitch! I can't bear it if King's Road win it.'

'They look as though they own it already,' Spag said grimly. White-clad figures were milling about on the grass and he could see the square shape of Thrasher, swaggering up and down.

With a squeak of brakes, the minibus pulled up on the gravel forecourt outside the house and Mr Fox turned round in the driving seat to look at the team.

'Right now, you lot, I want you all to behave like angels. Mr Grimes has been extraordinarily generous to lend the cricket pitch and have you all to tea afterwards. So no larking about. Right, Gobbo?'

'*Me?*' Barny looked hurt.

'All of you. Come on, now. I want to introduce you to Mr Grimes before the game starts.'

He got down to open the door. Climbing out, Clipper pulled at Barny's sleeve. 'Look, Gobbo, there's that old bloke in the wheelchair. The one who's always hanging about. What's he doing here?'

110

He was sitting in his chair on the gravel, grinning at them all. Barny shrugged. 'Dunno. He seems to get everywhere. Perhaps – '

But before he could finish, Mr Fox was leading them forwards. Towards the wheelchair. He smiled and shook the old man by the hand.

'Good afternoon, Mr Grimes. Very kind of you to have us.'

Barny gasped loudly. '*You're* Mr Grimes?'

Mr Fox glared at him, but the old man chuckled. 'Didn't expect it to be me, did you? What's the matter? Aren't I grand enough?'

'N-no,' stuttered Barny. 'I mean – it's not that. But I thought Mr Grimes would be really swish, with a Rolls-Royce and a chauffeur and – '

Mr Grimes snorted. 'Can't see much out of a Rolls-Royce, can you? I like to know what's going on around this town. And I do, don't I?' He winked at Barny and went on chuckling to himself as Mr Fox introduced the team. The chuckles did not stop until Denzil stepped forward. Then Mr Grimes looked startled and peered at him.

'Glad to see you here, boy,' he said gruffly. But he seemed thoughtful and, as they all started to move down the slope towards the cricket pitch, he beckoned Clipper closer to him.

'Here,' he muttered, 'that little lad, the one with the toothpaste. You haven't put him in the team just to keep him out of mischief, have you?'

'Of course not.' Clipper sounded shocked. 'We want to win and he's – well, you'll see.'

Mr Grimes gave a satisfied nod. 'Just as long

as you're not being soft with him. That one needs to be told straight when he's bad and when he's good.'

Clipper grinned. 'You'll see,' she said again, as she stepped on to the field.

Thrasher looked up and gave a loud laugh as he saw her coming. 'Oh, you've turned up. Didn't think you'd bother.'

Clipper's chin went up and she opened her mouth, but Spag was ready at her elbow.

'Don't bother,' he said quietly. 'He'll learn.'

Clipper relaxed and, puzzled, Thrasher looked round for another victim. His face brightened as he saw Denzil.

'Well, well. Batman. What's the matter, Clipper? Couldn't your blind player make it?'

But Denzil just gave a feeble smile and stayed silent. Before Thrasher could have a go at anyone else, he and Clipper were called over to take the toss.

'Heads,' came Clipper's clear voice.

'Tails!' Thrasher shouted triumphantly. 'We'll bat. I want a decent innings and if you go first we'll only have about five to make.' He strutted off towards the boundary.

'Right, men.' Clipper called them all round her. 'Thrasher's the one we've got to get. He'll go in first and hog the batting and, if we let him, he'll knock up a big score. We've got thirty overs today, so I think we should let him have his head for three or four overs. Let him get really cocky. Then, with any luck, he'll hit a nice, juicy catch.'

112

The others nodded, but Spag held up a warning hand. 'Watch those runs, though. I'll signal to you if I think he's getting too many.'

Clipper nodded confidently. 'OK. But don't worry. I know him. He can't resist showing off. Laurie, you bowl first, and we'll have Shane up at the other end.'

She directed the rest of the fielders and the game began with Laurie bowling a straight, slowish ball to Thrasher.

At once, Barny knew that Clipper had got it wrong. Normally, Thrasher would have plunged in from the start and given that ball a hefty swipe. But this game was important. There was something good to be won, and Thrasher intended to win it. So he was not taking any chances. He spent the first two or three balls carefully getting used to the wicket and the bowling and, when he did start to make runs, he was more cautious than usual. The score mounted steadily and Barny began to chew his fingers.

He could see Spag over by the scoreboard, frowning as he marked the runs down, and Clipper was looking nervously at Thrasher. After five overs, the score was twenty runs and Spag was pulling faces at them. Barny nudged Clipper at the end of the over.

'You've got to *do* something. Otherwise they'll make about a hundred and fifty.'

Clipper nodded thoughtfully. 'Mmm. Made a mistake, didn't I? We're not going to get Thrasher out in a hurry. But we might do something with the other one. He's getting quite twitchy, because Thrasher's hogging the bowling. Perhaps I'll have a bowl in a minute.'

Before she began, she had a mutter to Spotty McGrew, who was fielding on the boundary. Then she sent an easy ball to Thrasher. He swung at it and began to run, clearly expecting to score a four. But Spotty got to it, just before it reached the line. Thrasher had been trapped into taking three, and the other batsman was facing the bowling.

Clipper spat on her hands, rubbed the ball hard on her trousers, leaving a long, red smear, and came hurtling down towards him, with her teeth bared. He blinked, missed the ball and groaned as it bounced off his pad.

'Howzat?' Clipper shouted joyfully.

'You fool!' shouted Thrasher.

That made Clipper grin even more. If Thrasher lost his temper, her job would be easier.

But it was not as easy as that. The wickets had begun to fall, but Thrasher stayed firmly in position, still playing sensibly. At the end of twenty-five overs, the score was ninety-five, and Spag was waving his arms about and pointing frantically at the scoreboard.

'It's no good,' Clipper muttered to Barny as they waited for the eighth batsman. 'We've *got* to get Thrasher out. He could make another twenty or thirty runs.'

Barny pulled a face. 'And you don't think we can beat that? Not even with Denzil?'

Clipper glanced anxiously over at mid-on, where

Denzil stood, looking very pale. 'He's not exactly bouncy today, is he? Perhaps he's ill. Or he's lost his nerve. He's only a little boy, after all. We can't pin everything on him. We've got to get Thrasher out.'

The eighth batsman was a small, solid boy. He looked fearfully at Clipper and braced himself for a fast ball. But she bowled quite slowly, so that he was able to hit it and take a single.

'Yah!' shouted Thrasher as he ran. 'What a feeble ball!'

But Clipper only smiled to herself.

In the next few minutes, everything happened so quickly that Barny could not take it in. Clipper bared her teeth and came charging down from the far end. The ball whistled down the wicket, much faster than anything she had bowled so far. With a sneer, Thrasher stepped out to hit it. But it caught the edge of his bat and sailed up into the air, over his head, moving sideways and backwards.

'Gobbo!' yelled Clipper.

Thrasher glanced scornfully over his shoulder and began to run. Straining every muscle, Barny leaped for the ball, but although he tipped it with his fingers he could not grasp it, and he fell to the ground in an ungainly heap.

But suddenly everyone was cheering. Because the ball had fallen forward on to the wicket. Thrasher was run out for sixty-five and King's Road had made ninety-six.

'Right, men,' yelled Clipper. 'We've got them now!'

It took only three overs and eight runs. As the last wicket fell, Clipper raced round, banging the other fielders on the back.

But when they came off the field, they found Spag looking very gloomy. 'No use gloating,' he scowled. 'We've got to make a hundred and five, and we've *never* had a three figure total.'

'We've never had Denzil before,' Barny pointed out.

Spag looked even more miserable. 'Haven't you seen him? He looks as though he's about to drop down dead.'

Mr Grimes, who was sitting beside Spag, nodded in agreement. 'Been watching him, I have. He's properly got the wind up.'

Denzil did look bad. As though he were about to be sick. He came trailing across the grass towards Clipper and said. 'I don't really have to go in first, do I? *Please.*'

'But we agreed – ' began Clipper, frowning. Then she peered at him again and nodded. 'OK. Perhaps you'd better have a rest. You can go in number four.'

Mr Grimes opened his mouth. Then he shut it again.

'Shane,' Clipper went on, 'you can go in with Spotty. Don't worry. I don't expect a vast score. Just play steadily and let Spotty get the runs. He'll start us off OK.'

But she was wrong. Spotty was as nervous as everyone else. He spent the first two overs fumbling about, missing more balls than he hit and scoring only four. At the beginning of the third over, he tried to pull himself together, lashed out at a fast ball from Thrasher and was caught at mid-off.

Clipper bit back her anger. 'Tough luck, Spotty,' she said, as he came drooping back. 'Bet you were dying to hit Thrasher's bowling all over the field.'

'Not just his bowling,' Spotty said savagely. 'His head. He's out there gloating.'

Mr Grimes chuckled. 'Never mind, lad. Happens to us all. I scored a duck in the most important match of my life. You come over and watch with me.'

Slightly soothed, Spotty took off his pads and threw them to Denzil before going to sit by the wheelchair. Denzil started to put them on, staring over at Martin Grant, who was going out to bat. Barny saw his hands shaking as he did up the buckles and he decided it was time to cheer him up.

'Won't be long now. The waiting's always the worst part, isn't it?' Denzil nodded dumbly and Barny tried again. 'Shouldn't be more than an over or so before one of those two is out. *Then* you can show Thrasher. Eh?'

Denzil nodded again, but he did not even look pleased. Just went on staring out at the pitch. Barny looked at Spag and Clipper and pulled a worried face.

He was even more worried a quarter of an hour later. Because Shane and Martin were still there. They seemed to be paralysed with nerves. They were playing very, very carefully. Too carefully to be out. But too carefully to score runs either. At the end of ten overs, the score was only twenty, and Clipper was fuming and biting her fingers.

'The idiots! They're wasting time! We've only got twenty overs left now, and we've got eighty-five to score. It's *impossible*.'

At that moment, Shane stepped out to hit the ball, dithered, missed it and was stumped. Denzil stood up.

'Well, here goes.' He gulped.

Clipper looked kindly at him. 'Don't worry,' she said, with a visible effort. 'It's only a game. We won't eat you if we don't win.'

Beside her, she heard Mr Grimes snort strangely.

Denzil seemed very small as he walked out on to the pitch, with his knees knocking and his bat trailing. When he was halfway to the wicket, Mr Grimes suddenly gripped the arms of his wheelchair and yelled at the top of his voice.

'Might as well give up now, son. You're not big enough to do any good! Better go back to playing Batman!'

'What?' Clipper whirled at him, furious. 'What do you think you're doing?'

He grinned at her. 'I'm not daft. Told you not to treat that one too soft, didn't I? You've got him all of a dither, being kind to him. And he won't do anything unless he's angry. Look.'

Denzil's head had gone up and his face had turned very pink. He squared his shoulders and marched the rest of the way at top speed.

'Now,' said Mr Grimes quietly, 'the bowler

118

should do the rest for us. I hope he doesn't let us down.'

Thrasher put his hands together and clapped sarcastically. 'Poor little thing. Does it want me to bowl underarm, then? Diddums!'

'Oh, well done,' muttered Mr Grimes. 'Knew he'd do his stuff. Young Batman'll be OK now.'

Denzil was certainly fiery red. He did not answer Thrasher. Just tapped his bat on the ground and looked attentively at the bowling end.

Thrasher did not bowl like Clipper, with a long,

steady run. He came up quite slowly until the last few yards, paused slightly and then flung himself, arms and legs flailing furiously as the ball left his hand at high speed. It was a distracting sight which made it difficult for a new batsman to keep his eye on the ball.

But Denzil did not waste any time staring at Thrasher. He stepped forward, swung his bat and drove neatly to the boundary for four.

Thrasher's face was a lovely sight. His mouth dropped open. His eyes popped. 'Yah!' he yelled, 'What a fluke. I'll have your stumps next time, Batman.'

Denzil hit that ball for four in the other direction.

Spag wriggled his knees under the scorebook. 'You know, I'm just beginning to enjoy myself.'

'Told you it was easy to handle Denzil,' Barny said smugly. 'Told you we only needed to find something he liked doing.'

Clipper knocked him over absentmindedly and sat on his chest. 'Hope Martin has enough sense to let Denzil keep the batting. We've got to score fast and – oh, good shot, Denzil!' Forgetting where she was sitting, she bounced up and down excitedly.

'You thinking of growing up to be an elephant?' groaned Barny. 'Get off, Clipper. D'you want me to be a physical wreck, so I can't bat?'

'Gosh!' Clipper looked tragic. 'You mean – we might have to manage without you? We'd have no chance of winning then. Sob. Weep.'

'You might need him, at that,' Mr Grimes said.

'That Martin's got himself out already. That's a catch if ever I saw one.'

'Yikes!' Clipper rolled on to the grass as the ball cracked into Thrasher's hands. 'I'm in next, and I haven't got my pads on.'

It took her a couple of minutes to do up the buckles and all the time Thrasher was shouting, 'You scared then, Clipper? Can't face my bowling? You can give up now, if you like.'

'You *dare* lose this match,' Mr Grimes said, with controlled rage. 'If you do, I'll have to give my cricket pitch to King's Road. And I *will not* have that lout playing on it again.'

Clipper grinned at him. 'Do my best.'

But it was soon clear that Clipper was not out to make a lot of runs. She quickly took a single and let Denzil face the bowling. The score began to mount again and Mr Grimes leaned back in his wheelchair with an expression of deep pleasure.

'It's a joy to watch that boy bat. He's a natural. What's the score now?'

Spag glanced down his neat columns of figures. 'Sixty. We've only got another forty-five to make and I think we might just do it. There's twelve overs to go and we've got seven – oh no! We've only got six wickets.'

Clipper was on her way back to them, looking like thunder.

'Brilliant,' said Spotty. 'You beat me by one run.'

Clipper sank down on to the grass. 'It's the lowest score I've made since I was eight,' she said gloomily. 'I'm not sure we deserve to win.'

'Nonsense!' said Mr Grimes sharply. 'That's defeatist talk. Call yourself a captain?'

'Sorry.' Clipper sat up straight. 'You're right. We're doing OK. And we *can* win. As long as someone manages to stay in with Denzil. I just hope we don't get down to Gobbo.'

'Charming!' said Barny.

But a bit of him agreed with her. He did not like the look of Thrasher's bowling today. Not at all. So he dug his fingernails into the palms of his hands and wished, as the runs mounted and the wickets fell. Suddenly, Clipper leaned forward and clapped her hands hard.

'A hundred!' Jumping to her feet, she did a dance of joy on the boundary. 'We only need five more. We *must* do it! There's two wickets left and nearly an over to go and – oh, *Jimmy*!'

With the second ball of the last over, Thrasher had taken Jimmy Brown's wicket. Clipper caught at Barny's shoulder and squeezed it hard.

'It's you, Gobbo. And you mustn't let us down. All you've got to do is go in and *get a single*. So Denzil can have the bowling.'

'No problem,' Barny swaggered. He stuck out his stomach and strode on to the field.

'Right, Gobbo,' shouted Thrasher. 'I'm going to get you.' He was not jeering any more. He was very angry, because of what Denzil had been doing to his bowling. The first ball he sent down to Barny was fierce and fast and it came speeding towards him as if it would crack his bones.

Barny shuddered and did the only thing he knew

123

how to do with a ball like that. He held his bat steady and stopped it almost dead, jarring his arms. Over by the boundary, he could hear Clipper fizzing with disapproval. What did she expect? If he'd swiped at it, he'd probably be on his way to hospital. Anyway, there were three more balls left. If he took a single off the next one, Denzil would have two to make four runs.

But the next ball was even more ferocious. Automatically, even while he was trying to summon up enough courage to hit it, Barny blocked.

Clipper stood up and bellowed, '*Gobbo!* There's only two balls left. *You must hit this one!*'

Spag reached up an arm and pulled her down on to the grass again, but she went on waving her fists.

Barny looked from her to Thrasher, who was beginning his run, and then back again. Thrasher was terrifying, but Barny knew who scared him more. Clipper in a temper was no joke.

As the ball came zooming towards him, he said a quick prayer, shut his eyes and swung. The ball crashed against the wood of the bat and Barny began to run, blindly, with his eyes fixed on the ground.

When he got to the other end of the wicket, he bumped into Denzil. 'What? You idiot!' he shouted. 'You'll be out. You've got to run.'

'Nope,' said Denzil chirpily. 'I won't.'

'Don't be so rotten! We'll lose, and – '

'You are *dumb*.' Denzil grinned. 'We've won.'

'What?' Barny said again. Then he realised that everyone was cheering. Mr Grimes was clapping

124

his hands and banging Clipper on the back. And Thrasher was stamping off the pitch. 'What happened?'

Denzil laughed. 'You hit a six, thicko.'

Barny flung his bat into the air and charged towards Clipper. 'See? I told you I'd do it. I've won us the cricket pitch.'

'You?' shrieked Clipper.

'You?' spluttered Spag.

'Well – ' Barny began. He was just going to give Denzil a bit of the credit when Denzil himself arrived, pulling something out of his pocket.

'Yes, you, Gobbo,' he yelled. 'Congratulations!'

Sticking his hands out, he squeezed the tube of toothpaste he was holding. A great stream of green shot out all over Barny's shirt, Spag's glasses, Clipper's hair and Mr Grimes's wheelchair.

'Oh *no*!' groaned Spag. 'I'll *never* get my calculator. It's over a week till Aunt Rachel and Uncle Gregory get back.'

'Yes,' said Denzil happily. 'And I've got another four years eleven months and six days' supply of toothpaste left. BATMAN!'

Also by Gillian Cross

SAVE OUR SCHOOL

Bennett School isn't the best school in the world, but Clipper, Spag and Barny are sure it's a lot better than the school they'll have to go to if Bennett is knocked down. So, with their unusual talents they draw up an astonishing plan of action to save the school. But all their stunts seem to go wrong somehow, and it looks as if Bennett School will be knocked down after all . . .

Gillian Cross

SWIMATHON!

For the first time ever, Barny Gobbo is stuck for a Good Idea – just when money is urgently needed to repair the school minibus. The answer comes when a rival school issues a team swimming challenge. But Barny has reckoned without the bombshell Clipper and Spag are about to drop . . .